THE BOYS AND GIRLS BOOK
ABOUT STEPFAMILIES

The *stepfamily* is not a new phenomenon on the American scene. In fact, it has always been quite common. However, in past centuries it was generally the result of parental death; in this century parental divorce has been the main cause. Just as the rate of divorce involving children has increased markedly in recent years, so has the rate of remarriage involving children. *THE BOYS AND GIRLS BOOK ABOUT STEPFAMILIES* is for all these young children and their parents.

As with Dr. Gardner's other highly praised books (*THE BOYS AND GIRLS BOOK ABOUT DIVORCE, THE PARENTS BOOK ABOUT DIVORCE,* and *THE BOYS AND GIRLS BOOK ABOUT ONE-PARENT FAMILIES*), the emphasis throughout is on honesty about feelings and on learning to communicate them in appropriate and constructive ways, all in a reassuring and commonsense style.

D0004865

Other books by Richard A. Gardner, M.D.

THE BOYS AND GIRLS BOOK ABOUT STEPFAMILIES

Richard A. Gardner, M.D.

Clinical Professor of
Child Psychiatry
Columbia University,
College of Physicians and Surgeons

Illustrations by
Alfred Lowenheim

Creative Therapeutics
155 County Road   Cresskill, N.J. 07626-0317

THE BOYS AND GIRLS BOOK
ABOUT STEPFAMILIES

Bantam Books Edition, February 1982
First Creative Therapeutics Edition, June 1985

Illustrations by Alfred Lowenheim

ISBN 0-933812-13-2

PRINTED IN THE UNITED STATES OF AMERICA

0   9   8   7   6   5   4   3

To
my late brother,
Ronald M. Gardner
and my parents,
Amelia and Irving Gardner

CONTENTS

ACKNOWLEDGMENTS

First, I wish to express my gratitude to Toni Burbank, executive editor at Bantam Books, who was most receptive to my suggestion that there was a need for a book such as this. Her concern, interest, and assistance with the original manuscript are most appreciated. My secretary, Mrs. Linda Gould, as usual, dedicated herself to the typing of the manuscript. Mrs. Frances Dubner, as always, edited the manuscript with enthusiasm and devotion. Her advice was sensitive and extremely helpful. As I am sure the readers will agree, I am deeply indebted to Al Lowenheim for his unusual artistic talent. Al has a way of portraying the most painful experiences in such a way that optimism usually creeps through and a successful outcome seems almost inevitable. I am grateful, as well, to Colette Conboy for her dedication to the publication of the Creative Therapeutics edition.

My greatest debt of all is to the children, parents, and stepparents who have taught me so much about life in the stepparent home. My hope is that what I have learned from their pains and frustrations will prove useful in helping others prevent and alleviate theirs.

INTRODUCTION
FOR PARENTS
AND STEPPARENTS

I am sure that all of you are aware of the fact that in recent years there has been a dramatic increase in the rate of divorce in this country. What you may not realize is that the large majority of divorced people remarry, often bringing children from an earlier marriage into their new home. This has led to more and more stepfamily households, making stepfamilies much more common than they once were. The challenges and difficulties of starting a new family with growing children have not become easier to meet just because they are more common. I have written this book for your children and stepchildren in the hopes that it might help them adjust to their new families. The success of *The Boys and Girls Book About Divorce* and *The Boys and Girls Book About One-Parent Families* helped convince me that a similar volume for children living in stepfamilies might also be useful.

This book has been written primarily for children in the six- to twelve-year age group. It is written so that the average eight- to nine-year-old can read it alone and understand it. Children as young as five will gen-

1

erally understand most of what is written here if it is read to them. Although not specifically written for adolescents, many of the issues I discuss throughout the book are relevant to this age group. Many adolescents may consider the book "childish" and be reluctant to read it, but if they can overcome initial reservations, most of them will find that there is a great deal of information that can be useful to them. Because I am concerned with how the stepfamily can solve its own problems, I have included information that you as a parent or stepparent can use to help the children adjust to their changed family. If you decide to read this book along with your child or children, you may find that the experience can enrich your family relationships since the issues raised can serve as starting points for family discussions. These discussions can contribute significantly to improved family communication and the prevention of some common family and stepfamily misunderstandings.

Above all, this is a practical book. Its purpose is to tell children *how* to deal with some of the common problems that new stepfamilies encounter. It not only tells them *why* certain things happen but *what* they can do to avoid and relieve difficulties. It encourages positive adjustment through understanding and action. I have presented such questions as what to call a stepparent, how to deal with angry feelings, loyalty fights, common fears in the new situation, differences in family rules, and coping with stepsiblings. Of course, not every child will find that each new situation causes a problem in his family, and I urge parents and children to scan the table of contents and refer to those sections that interest and concern them.

I have deliberately chosen to retain the term *stepfamily* in this book rather than use such recently introduced substitutes as *blended* families and *reconstituted* families, which have been introduced because of the poor reputation that the term *step* has come to have. Actually, there is nothing intrinsically denigrating about the word step; it has just come to be associated with words like mean and cruel. The term *step* is derived from an Old English term meaning bereaved or deprived. Prior to a century ago, most parents became single because of the death of their spouses rather than divorce. Divorce was extremely uncommon and often impossible. Because most people died at ages younger than they do now, the death of a spouse was the cause of single parenthood in the overwhelming majority of cases. A stepparent, then, replaced a dead parent, and a stepchild was a child whose parent had died.

As modern medicine increased our expected life spans and as divorce laws became more liberalized, most single parents were divorced rather than widowed. Today, the term *stepparent* has come to mean the spouse of a remarried parent. It also indicates that there is no blood relationship between the child and the new spouse. It is used to refer to three situations: (1) remarriage after death of a parent, (2) remarriage after parental divorce, and (3) the marriage of a parent who has never previously been married. Another way of viewing it is to consider it to be *one step away* from natural parenthood. In *The Parents Book About Divorce*, I discussed in detail what I believe to be important factors

3

that have contributed to the stepparents' (especially the stepmother's) poor reputation. In this book, I will provide your child with some insight into this unfortunate phenomenon. My hope is that such understanding will help to dispel this sad and destructive myth.

The myth of the evil stepparent is not the only one I attempt to dispose of in this book. My hope is that it will also dispel another common myth as well, namely, the myth of instant love. As enjoyable as "love at first sight" and other states of romantic euphoria may initially be, they are often based on fantasies about the beloved rather than on what kind of person the loved one actually is. Most mature people appreciate that such feelings do not last indefinitely and that a more stable, loving relationship can only evolve over time. Such a relationship can only have solidity when there is knowledge of what the beloved is really like and experience that confirms loving feelings and allows trust to grow.

It is not just adults who believe in "instant love"; often, children also think this is how love happens. It is vital for a healthy stepparent-stepchild relationship that children understand that love takes time to grow. Stepparents should avoid the seemingly benevolent but misguided stance that they love the stepchildren as much as their own. It is important to tell a child that true, healthy love does not rise instantaneously, that it develops over time and grows best when both people try to be as considerate of and as giving to one another as they possibly can. It is in this way that a loving relationship between stepparents and stepchildren becomes possible. In this book, I suggest to children how they can try to develop a loving relationship with their stepparent. I use the word *try* because no one can guarantee that even the most sincere efforts can elicit love. This holds true for love between natural children and their parents as well as between stepchildren and stepparents. Stepparents and parents can also help stepchildren understand that love is not an absolute but that there are many degrees of love.

Building the new family is primarily the responsibility of the adults, but there is much that the children can do. I encourage them to make their contributions and offer specific information and advice on how they can help make their new family a successful one. Again, this book can only provide understanding and suggestions; it cannot ensure success.

With the exception of one chapter, I do not make a distinction between families in which the parents are unmarried and living together and those in which the parents are married. Psychologically, there is little (but certainly some) difference between the two situations. One problem that may arise when unmarried parents live together is parental shame, especially that of the mother. If a woman has been brought up in a traditional home where living together with a man without being married to him was something that was done only by the "lowest" sorts of women, she may be beset by conflicting emotions. While there is now far less societal disapproval about living together than there was even a few years ago, some women still feel guilty about living in an unmarried home even when they realize that it is the best arrangement for them.

Those women who experience some guilt and embarrassment, do well not only to accept these feelings but also to have faith in the very real benefits they hope to gain for their new family. The best position for the mother to take with the children is to be honest with them, to explain why she is not presently marrying the man she is living with and what her future plans *might* be. She should make it clear that the new arrangement *is* a family. As long as she can convey her conviction that what she is doing is right for her family, the children are less likely to feel guilt, shame, or confusion when they are confronted by people outside the family. If guilt and embarrassment are her dominant emotions, the children are likely to respond similarly. One danger of these feelings is that the children will be asked to join a conspiracy of silence in which they are told not to reveal the arrangement to certain parties. If children are asked to hide the way they live, they are essentially being told that their mother is doing something bad. When the mother is forthright about her choice, she is in a better position to advise the children when, and if, they are subjected to criticism by their playmates or some adults. When they are exposed to criticism of the family, they should be helped to appreciate that the problem lies in the minds of those who criticize them rather than in themselves or the adults with whom they are living.

Although the stepfamily household has situations not present in the traditional first-marriage home, stepchildren need not necessarily develop psychological problems. The risk of some difficulties is greater in the stepfamily home because of the special adjustment problems that children must face in these families. This book has been written primarily to help prevent such problems. It may serve, as well, to alleviate some difficulties, but it should be understood that it can generally be of help only with the milder forms. More severe forms of psychological disturbance are not likely to be alleviated by books such as this; rather, psychotherapy of varying degrees of intensity and duration is often necessary.

Parents may wonder at this point how they can tell whether their children need therapy. It would take a completely different kind of book to discuss this in detail, but there are a few general comments I can make here that may prove useful. The poorest time to make a decision about the need for professional help is during the formation of the new family. Such periods are trying for all concerned, and inappropriate and atypical behavior is almost predictable (not only for the children but even for the adults). It is only after many months have passed that one is in a position to decide whether treatment is warranted. If a child is doing well in school (both academically and in the behavioral realm), *and* if the child has meaningful relationships with friends (seeks and is sought by peers), *and* if he or she does not present significant behavior problems at home (most children do to some degree), then it is unlikely that the child is having significant psychological difficulties. There are some children, however, who may appear to be functioning well in all of these areas but who still may be having problems. For example, there are children who exhibit certain symptoms such as tics, physical complaints of a psychological origin, fears, and anger inhibitions who may still be functioning well in all of

7

the aforementioned areas. This is uncommon, however. Most often, if a child exhibits one or more of these symptoms, he or she is also likely to be having trouble in school or the neighborhood or at home. The parent who suspects that a child may need treatment should seek the opinion of a mental health professional as to whether or not therapy is indicated.

There is one situation that a child who needs therapy may be in that I believe is worthy of special emphasis. I am referring to the situation in which both mother and father have either remarried or are living with new partners and yet continue the hostilities that originally led to their divorce. Each natural parent has gained an ally in the new spouse. A significant amount of time and energy may be spent by the adults in ongoing litigation and in other forms of hostile entanglement that adversely affect the child. A therapist who attempts to treat the child who has been caught in this network of hostility without seeing the adults as well may find that it is impossible to help the child. Work must be done as much as possible with all four adults as well as with the child if one is to expect real benefits to the family.

Family counseling may be a threat to the new spouses, for they may fear that working together again may bring the natural parents to a reconciliation. The new spouses should understand that this is not likely to occur (in my experience I have never seen it happen, although I must admit that it possibly could) and that the former spouses may still be married to one another in the psychological sense. For example, a therapist could reasonably say to a second wife, "Although you are legally married to your husband and he is legally divorced from his first wife, from the psychological point of view, he is still married to his first wife. If one were to have a printout of all his thoughts and one were to count those that relate to his first wife and compare that number to those thoughts that relate to you, his second wife, it is likely that the number would be greater for her than for you. If you are to participate, encourage, and support such counseling, there is a possibility that your husband may finally become psychologically a monogamist and fully your husband. However, this not only requires effort on the part of all parties but also involves a certain risk, albeit a small one. In any event, you not only have this to gain by your support and participation but, in addition, if you see things going in the direction that you fear, that is, that there may be a disruption of your relationship and a reconciliation with his former wife, you can then withdraw your support and/or remove yourself from involvement in the therapy. If you decide to accept my invitation to become involved in the counseling, you will have an opportunity to change the situation or at least participate in such potential changes." I recognize that such counseling is novel, to say the least, and is quite threatening to many. It is, however, becoming ever more commonly utilized by therapists, because they recognize that it provides the greatest possibility for resolution of some of the more common kinds of problems that stepchildren manifest.

The guiding principle that runs throughout this book is that the best way to resolve difficulties is through open communication, mutual discussion, and hard work

among the family members. There are also times, however, when temporarily separating family members f ͻm
one another is the most helpful approach, times ⱱhen
the situation benefits from decompression ratʰ ⱼr than
further attempts at resolution. Mother may ⱼook forward to those weekends when her childⱼ en will be
visiting with their father. Her peace, however, does not
come if her new husband's children descend upon the
home for their weekend visit with their father. It is at
times valuable, and even crucial, for the parents to get
away from all children in order to preserve their sanity.
Similarly, children can also profit from weekend trips,
sleep-over parties, sleep-away camps, etc. The children
not only gain the immediate benefits of these activities
but also the fringe benefit of their parents' and stepparents' renewed vigor.

In recent years, we have heard much talk about how
the two-parent family does not deserve the fine reputation it enjoys. Some even consider the preference for
two parents over one to be based on irrational preju-
dice. But I still believe that the two-parent family is
preferable to the one-parent family. From the simple
vantage point of manpower (or "person power" if one
wishes to call it that), two adults can do a much better
job of raising children than one. Child rearing involves
extensive work, and it is useful to have more "hands."
In addition, having two parents, one of each sex, can
help the child learn during the formative years how to
relate to individuals of both sexes. It is harder to do
this in a one-parent family. The traditional family model
provides the child with a same-sex parent for identifi-
cation purposes and an opposite-sex parent to learn

10

how to relate successfully to the opposite sex in future courting, mating, and marriage. Because the stepfamily situation approximates this ideal, it is preferable, in my opinion, to the single-parent home. I assume that parents who buy this book for their children agree. It is my hope that this book will play a role in helping the stepfamily approximate, as much as possible, the traditional two-parent family, the kind of family that I believe is most likely to produce healthy, productive, and fulfilled parents and children.

INTRODUCTION
FOR BOYS AND GIRLS

My name is Dr. Richard Gardner. I am a child psychiatrist. For many years I have seen children whose families have broken up. I have also seen many children whose parents get married again or live with a friend. I know the kinds of thoughts and feelings children usually have in such situations—how scared and angry they often become and how confusing it all may be. Such children have also told me about many other feelings and thoughts they have, like shame, and sadness, and blaming themselves. Practically all children have these thoughts and feelings when there are such big changes in their lives. It's normal and natural to have them. As a child psychiatrist I try to help children deal with these new feelings and thoughts in the best possible ways.

Some of you may have read my *Boys and Girls Book About Divorce*. In that book, I try to help children with some of the troubles that they might have when parents get divorced. I hope that those of you who have read that book have found it useful. Just as divorce can sometimes cause children worry and sadness, a parent's getting married again to another person may sometimes cause problems. I say *may* because sometimes it does and sometimes it doesn't. In this book, I try to help children with the troubles they may have when parents live together with a new person or get married again to someone else. Most of these problems can be helped by children and their families if they understand them. In this book, I give you advice about how you can go about solving many of them. The more children try to help themselves, the greater the chances they will change the things that are troubling them.

If you are becoming part of a stepfamily, you have already gone through some big changes in your life. Your parents may have been divorced, or perhaps one of your parents died. You may have lived for several years with one of your parents, and visited with the other. You certainly have had to cope with a lot of new situations and new thoughts and feelings. Some of you who read this book may already have been living in a stepfamily for a long time. Perhaps you wish that you were happier in your stepfamily—or just more comfortable. Perhaps you have problems that seem too big for you to solve alone. This book is for you, too.

The first important thing for you to remember is that everybody—both children and adults—gets frightened of new situations. Although adults may be less scared because they have more experience, they still get frightened, even if only a little bit. But children are more likely to be scared because they have not had as much experience dealing with many different kinds of situations. I want you to understand that practically everyone is scared when a new family begins. Both the adults and the children are frightened, and this is normal. After all, no one knows what to expect. Meeting

13

people gives you some idea about what to expect, but it's only after you start to live with them that you really know what's going to happen.

Betty, for example, was very frightened when her mother told her that she was going to marry her friend Ray and that they would be living with Ray and his two sons, Rob and Scott. Betty liked Ray and his boys. She was an only child and liked the idea of having two brothers, but she was still scared. After her mother got married, Betty found out that the more she got used to living with Ray and his sons, the less scared she became. That's one of the ways in which fears go away. As time passes and we learn about a new situation and get used to it, we become less scared of it.

Some children fear that they will lose a parent when there is a new marriage. One boy named Ronald thought that now that his mother was marrying a new husband, he would no longer see his father. When he spoke to people about his fears, he found out that they weren't true. And when he continued to see his father after his mother got married again, Ronald knew for sure that they weren't true. So talking about your fears and getting more information about what you are afraid of can lessen them. Having experiences can also help lessen fears.

One of the biggest worries that children have about a new marriage is that the parent they now live with will spend less time with them. This is especially true when the new person also has children. This is a reasonable fear to have. It is usually true that a parent will spend less time with a child after a new marriage, but this doesn't mean that there will be no time at all for the

14

child. Later on in this book, I will talk much more about this kind of fear and what can be done about it.

Some children are scared that the parent they live with will no longer love them and that the parent will only love the new husband or wife. This doesn't usually happen. Love is not like a piece of pie, where there is only a certain amount to go around. It is like a spring of water that is always filling up and always has water for lots of people. Later on, I will talk more about love and show you what you can do to be sure that you get as much of it as possible.

One of the biggest worries that children have before a parent marries again is that the new parent, the stepparent, will be mean to them. Even if they know the person well and he or she has not yet been mean, they may still fear that it will happen. Although it sometimes happens, often it does not. In this book, I will talk about the things children can sometimes do to prevent it from happening.

The worries and fears I have just spoken about are normal. They are to be expected, and I cannot imagine a child's not having at least some of them. Most of the things I will be talking about in this book are the normal and usual kinds of problems that most children are bound to have. Having problems does not mean that you are different or bad or crazy. It does not mean that you need special treatment or other help. Most of the problems I will be talking about in this book are the everyday kinds that can be solved by the people themselves.

The first thing that you have to do in order to solve a problem is to accept the fact that there *is* a problem.

15

Some people, both young and old, will make believe that a problem doesn't exist when it really does. This may make them feel better at first. But the trouble doesn't go away and may even get worse. Later, such people are often sorry that they didn't think about the problem and try to do something about it. I hope that you aren't doing this. If you are, now is the time to stop. Now is the time to look at your troubles without trying to make believe that they aren't there. This book was written to help you look at stepfamily problems so that you can do something about them.

This may not be an easy book for you to read. Some of the things I say are hard to understand even for adults. You will probably find it is best to read it a little bit at a time. You may also find that you will want to read only certain parts. This is fine. You can still learn a lot by reading only the parts that discuss the things that you have questions about. However, it still might be a good idea to read the parts that you skipped over. There may be things there that might be of interest and use to you.

If you do not understand something that I say, try reading that part along with a grownup, especially your mother, father, stepmother, or stepfather. Since they are all part of your new family, they are the best ones to read with. But even more important than reading together is talking with your parents and stepparents about the things I say. Talking things over can be very useful. It not only helps you to worry less, but it can bring your parents, your stepparents, and your siblings and stepsiblings closer together. Trying to make the family work together can help make people more tender and loving.

Even more important than *talking about* what I say here is *doing* the things I suggest. Although this may be the hardest way to solve your problems, it's the best way. Only by trying the things I suggest and by practicing them will you be able to see if they can help you and your stepfamily.

There's an old saying: "Nothing ventured, nothing gained." This means that if you do not try something, you cannot enjoy the things that might happen if you did try. If you don't try, you can't possibly change anything. If you don't try, you're just where you were. If you don't try, then you might still have your old problems. If you do try, you might solve many of them. So I hope that you'll try out the things I suggest, and find that my advice has been useful and helpful.

1
WHAT IS A STEPFAMILY?

If your father is no longer married to your mother—
either because your parents have divorced or because
your mother has died—and then he marries again, his
new wife is called your *stepmother*. A stepmother may
never have been married before, or she may have been
divorced, or her previous husband may have died. Sometimes she has children, and sometimes she doesn't. If
she does, then her children are called your *stepbrothers*
and *stepsisters*. It doesn't matter whether you live with
her or not. As long as she is not your real or natural
mother and as long as she is married to your father,
she is your stepmother.

In the same way, a *stepfather* is a man who is not your
real father but is married to your mother. A stepfather
may never have been married before, or he may have
been divorced, or his previous wife may have died. If
he has children, they are your stepbrothers and stepsisters, whether or not you live with them.

When parents are each married for the first time,
their children are called brothers and sisters. They all
have the same mother *and* the same father. They are

called *full brothers* and *full sisters*. All together, they are said to be *full siblings*.

A stepbrother or stepsister is the child of your stepfather or stepmother. Stepbrothers and stepsisters are called *stepsiblings*. You and your stepsiblings have different mothers and different fathers. You do not share either the same mother or the same father with your stepsiblings. Stepsiblings are your relatives, however, because one of their parents is married to one of your parents.

When a father and stepmother or a mother and stepfather have a child, that child is called your *half brother* or *half sister*. Half brothers and half sisters are called *half siblings*. Your half siblings have one parent who is the same as yours and another parent who is your stepparent. Two half siblings may have the same mother and different fathers, or they may have the same father and different mothers. Half siblings are also your relatives. They are halfway between your full siblings and your stepsiblings.

Although the word *stepfamily* is usually used when one talks about people living together in the same house, you are still part of the stepfamily even if you do not live with your stepparent, stepsiblings, or half siblings. They are all your relatives. You are now part of two families. Even though you live with one family, you will usually visit the other, and you are part of that family, too. In this book, I will be talking mainly about children who are *living* with their stepparents and step siblings. However, most of the things I will be talking

about will also be true for children who are *visiting* their stepfamilies.

All this may seem very complicated to you. Well, it is. Even grownups sometimes get confused about all these different kinds of relationships. Perhaps this picture will help make things clearer. Here the woman in the family on the right, who is holding the baby, was married to the man in the family on the left, who is also holding a baby. They got divorced, and each one married another person who also had one or more children. The father on the right has brought his daughter from his first marriage to live with him. The mother on the left has brought her two sons from her first marriage to live with her. Then a child was born in each of the new marriages. The picture shows the parents of the old marriage, the stepparents of the new marriage, and all the siblings, stepsiblings, and half siblings. Look at the picture carefully and see if you can name each of these different kinds of children. If you are still not clear about all these different relationships, ask a grownup to read over this part of the book with you while giving the names of the different kinds of relatives you have. This should help you understand these relationships better.

WORDS LIKE STEPMOTHER AND STEPFATHER ARE NOT BAD WORDS

There are some people who do not like the words stepmother or stepfather. A woman may say to her new husband's children from his earlier marriage, "I never want you to call me your *step*mother." Or a man may say to his new wife's children from her previous marriage, "I never want you to call me your *step*father." To them, the *step* part of the word stepmother or stepfather means *cruel* or *mean*. They may not even like words like stepbrother, stepsister, or stepfamily. Now where did they get this idea—the idea that there is something bad about the word step? Before answering that question, I'd like to say some other things first.

About four hundred years ago, there lived in England a man named William Shakespeare. He wrote many great plays in which he said many wise things. I'm sure that many of you have heard of him. One of the plays he wrote was called *Hamlet*. In this play, the young prince Hamlet says, "There is nothing either good or bad, but thinking makes it so." This means that *how* you think about something makes it good or bad to you. If you are taught to believe that something is

21

good, it will seem good to you. And if you are brought up to believe that something is bad, it will seem bad to you. The word step is just one example of this. The word step is neither good nor bad. If we think it's bad, it will become bad to us, and if we think it's not bad, it won't bother us. So we learn from William Shakespeare that a thing is bad only if we think it's bad and good if we believe it to be so.

Up until about a hundred years ago, very few people got divorced. The laws made it very hard to get a divorce, or sometimes even impossible. In spite of this, many children still lived with only one parent. The reason was that people died then at a much younger age than they do now. Not only did many more children die before they grew up, but also parents died before their children grew up.

Now you may be wondering what this has to do with the word step. In olden times, step meant *deprived*, that is, someone who is sad over the death of a person he or she liked or loved. A stepchild was a child whose mother or father had died. A stepmother was a woman who married a father whose wife had died. A stepfather was a man who married a mother whose husband had died.

In olden days, children with a stepparent usually had only one of their original parents still living. They were children who had lost their real mother or father. Today, most children with stepparents have *both* of their real parents still living. Today, most stepfamilies are formed after parents get divorced, not because a parent has died. This is a very big difference between children in olden days and children today. This is one of the reasons why children today are luckier than those who lived in former times. Children today whose parents get divorced and married again still have both original parents, as well as their new stepparent or stepparents.

So we see that in olden days, the word step just meant that something sad had happened in the family—a parent had died. How, then, did stepparents get to be considered mean? The idea that they are mean is not a new one. Fairy tales are hundreds of years old, and in many of them, stepmothers are very cruel. You probably know the story of Hansel and Gretel, where the stepmother tries to leave the children in the woods to starve to death. Cinderella's stepmother didn't want her to go to the ball. Instead, she wanted her own daughters to go in the hope that one of them would marry the handsome prince. And Snow White's stepmother—in the disguise of a witch—tried to kill her by feeding her a poisoned apple. So fairy tales helped give people the idea that stepmothers are mean. But these are just old made-up stories. They were made up to be as exciting and scary as possible. In fact, the scarier they were, the more people liked them. Things like this hardly ever happened then *or* now. Stepmothers don't go around leaving their stepchildren in the woods to starve to death. And they can't change into witches who feed their stepchildren poisoned apples. Although no one really believed that these fairy tales were true, they still helped people get the idea that stepparents are mean.

Another reason why stepparents came to be seen as cruel is that they usually do not, at first, love their stepchildren as much as their own children. This is something that many people do not like to talk about, but it is still quite true. However, this should not be surprising. A real mother carried her baby in her belly for nine months before it is born. She may have fed the baby from her own breasts. She has known the baby from the day it was born. Although a father doesn't carry the child in his belly, it was his sperm that made it start growing. He has usually thought about and loved the baby even while it was inside the mother. He could feel it kicking by feeling his wife's belly. And he shared with the mother the joy of its birth. Both he and the mother enjoyed cuddling and playing with the newborn infant. They both enjoyed seeing the baby learn to walk, talk, and grow older.

On the other hand, stepchildren come to stepparents at many different ages, and they are usually much older than newborn infants when stepparents first meet them. Stepparents cannot be expected to love children

they have just met as much as those they have known for many years. But this does not mean that they don't love them at all.

Some people don't realize that there are different amounts of love that people can have for one another. They think that either you love someone completely or you don't love the person at all. They do not realize that love can grow from a little to a lot. Some people think that stepparents who do not love their stepchildren as much as their own children are cruel. This is not true. It's natural, and it doesn't necessarily mean that the stepparent is cruel. However, as time goes on, stepparents *can* love their stepchildren more and more. It may even happen that stepparents may come to love their stepchildren as much as their own children. But even if a stepparent does not reach that point, it does not mean that the stepparent is cruel or mean.

So that's how it happened. That's how people got to believe that stepmothers and stepfathers are mean. They believed those fairy tale stories, and thought that real stepparents would be as cruel as Hansel and Gretel's stepmother or as mean as Cinderella's stepmother. And they believed in another fairy tale, that there is "love at first sight."

In real life, true love can come only after time, only after people have gotten to know one another. In real life, some children's own mothers and fathers are mean and cruel. And there are also mean stepmothers and cruel stepfathers. But this doesn't mean that *all* stepparents are cruel. Many are very loving, and if the child is nice to them, there is a good chance of getting even more love from them. Most stepparents want to

love their stepchildren. And most are *fair* even if they don't love their stepchildren as much as their own. Most try to be kind, giving, and tender to their stepchildren. Most want to have a nice family life and to have fun times. Most know, however, that in real life things are never perfect and that no family is perfect, not even one in which there has never been a divorce. In every family, there are times when there are fights. In every family, there are times when people love one another less than at other times. This is true of stepfamilies as well.

It is very important to remember that the names people use with one another—whether it is a step name or any other kind of name—do not determine whether they love one another. The way they *feel* about each other and how they *act* with one another tell whether there is true love. Love is a feeling that can only come after two people have been nice to each other over a period of time. It does not come quickly. It cannot come from being called a certain name; nor can a name make it go away.

2
WHEN A PARENT LIVES WITH AN UNMARRIED PARTNER

Sometimes a parent lives with another person without being married. There is no special name like stepfamily that everybody had agreed to use for these families. They usually look like stepfamilies, and most of their experiences are the same as those that people have when parents are married. Because of this, I will be calling these families *stepfamilies* as well even though I know that the word is really not completely correct. The important thing is that they *are* really families. In this chapter, I am giving special attention to this kind of family, but remember that whenever I use the word stepfamily, I am talking about families in which the parents are not married as well as families in which the parents are married.

WHAT TO DO WHEN PEOPLE CRITICIZE YOUR PARENT FOR LIVING WITH SOMEONE

There are some people who believe that it is wrong for a man and a woman to live together without being married. They believe that it is bad or sinful. Many years ago, most people thought this way, but most people now believe that it is perfectly all right. I, myself, do not think that there is anything wrong with two people living together without being married. More and more people are doing so these days. It's just one of many possible ways people can live together. But because some people still have old-fashioned ideas, there are some children who are made to feel ashamed that a parent is living with a friend without being married.

Sometimes other children might try to make you feel ashamed. Young children usually believe the same things as their parents. If a parent believes that there is something wrong with people living together without being married, their children are likely to believe the same thing. These children may make fun of other children whose parents are living together without being married. They may tease them and call them bad names. They may even say bad things about the adults who are living together. There is something wrong with children who go around making fun of others and calling them bad names. They are being cruel.

So if this has happened to you or if it happens to you someday, think about what I have just said. Remember that there is nothing wrong with what your parent and his or her friend are doing. There is, however, something wrong with the person who is calling you names. The problem lies in that person's head, not in anything you or your parent or your parent's friend is doing. It is perfectly all right for you to tell this person you think he or she is not only stupid and foolish but also mean and cruel.

29

Some parents who live together with another person want it kept a secret that they are not married. They may be afraid of what others might say. They may even ask the child to keep it a secret. I believe that this is a big mistake. It is not fair to ask children to try to keep this secret. You may go around scared that the secret will slip out, or you might start to feel ashamed of what your parent is doing. All this may add new worries.

So if your parent is asking you to keep this secret, tell him or her that trying to keep the secret gives you an extra worry. Try to get your parent to change his or her mind. Tell your parent how it makes you go around scared that the secret will slip out. You might even want to show your parent what I say here.

This is what happened to Sally. Sally's mother decided to invite her friend Mike to live with them. Sally's

mother and Mike loved each other very much, but they didn't know whether or not they wanted to get married. Each had been married before, and they wanted to be sure not to make the same mistake again. Sally's grandparents, her mother's parents, lived in a distant city. Sally used to talk to her grandparents on the telephone about once a week. They also wrote each other letters. Sally loved her grandparents very much, and her grandparents loved Sally very much. In fact, they used to call her their "pride and joy."

On the day that Mike moved in, Sally's mother said to her, "Sally, it's very important that you not let Grandma and Grandpa know about Mike's living with us. They wouldn't understand, and it would make them upset."

Sally then asked her mother, "Why should they be upset?"

Her mother answered, "Well, there's really nothing to be upset about, but they're old people, and they have old-fashioned ideas, and they would think it's wrong. If we tell them, they'll feel bad."

Sally was really confused by what her mother had said. If there was really nothing wrong with what her mother and Mike were doing, why shouldn't her grandparents know about it? Why should she have to keep it a secret? Sally didn't tell her mother how confused she was about what was going on because she wanted to be a good girl and listen to her mother.

And so each time she talked to her grandparents on the phone, she became quite frightened. She was scared that the secret might slip out. Soon she thought it would be safer not to speak to her grandmother or grandfather at all. Even her letters became shorter because she was afraid to write anything that might tell about Mike.

One day, her grandmother called, and Sally just refused to go to the phone. Her grandmother got very upset and wanted to know why Sally hadn't written and why Sally didn't even want to talk to her. Sally got so upset that she just started crying. Her mother told her grandmother that she would call her back later, and she asked Sally what was wrong. Sally then told her mother how scared she was to speak or write to her grandparents because she feared she might let out the secret about Mike.

Sally's mother then realized that she had made a big mistake. She told Sally that she had been foolish. She told her that she was going to tell Sally's grandparents about Mike and explain her decision to them.

Sally's mother called the grandmother back and told her the whole story. To Sally's mother's surprise, the grandmother was not as upset as Sally's mother thought she would be. She was a little upset but quickly got used to the idea. Sally was sorry that she hadn't spoken up sooner and was glad that she had finally done so.

WHAT TO CALL THE PERSON WHO LIVES WITH YOUR PARENT

When parents are married to the person with whom they are living, the new person is called either a stepmother or a stepfather. There is no special name that is used everywhere for the person who lives with someone without being married. The word I have already used is *friend*. It is a word that you might choose to use.

It is certainly shorter than *the man my mother lives with* or *the woman my father lives with*. However, to refer to the person as simply a friend does not tell whether or not the parent is living with that person. So the word friend does not solve completely the problem of what to call that person.

Sometimes the word *boy friend* and *girl friend* are used. This is fine when the two people are young and have never been married before. However, people who have been married before and have children are usually full-grown adults. They are no longer boys or girls. So I don't like to use such words for the adults we are talking about here.

When two people are planning to get married, the words *fiancé* and *fiancée* are used. (Both of these words are pronounced the same: fee-on-SAY.) The man is the fianc*é*; the woman is the fianc*ée*. But these words still do not tell whether or not the two people are living together. Also, some people who live together do not plan to marry, and others are living together in order to help them decide whether or not they should get married. In these cases, the words fiancé and fiancée should not be used.

In recent years, some people have suggested that the two people in this situation refer to one another as *mates* or *housemates*. The word mate is a good one because it can be used for both the man and the woman, and that makes it easier to use. The word housemate tells that the two people live together. Even though housemate may be a good word, not too many people have used it, and many people would not understand what you were talking about if you were to use it.

It seems, then, that at this time we don't have many good choices. We need a better word to describe two people who are living together in the same house. Until we get such a word, and I believe we will, my first choice is *friend*, and my second choice is *the woman my father lives with* or *the man my mother lives with*. It might be best to talk this over with your parent and see what word he or she is using.

The question of what names you should call the person with whom your parent lives is a more difficult one. There is no really good, easy answer to this question.

Let us take, for example, the situation in which a divorced mother is living with her son Daniel. She meets a man named Robert Smith. Mr. Smith's friends call him Rob, and the people he meets in his work call him Mr. Smith. When your mother first introduces you to him, she might say, "Daniel, I'd like you to meet my friend, Mr. Robert Smith," or, "I'd like you to meet my friend, Rob Smith." After that, you might be calling him *Mr. Smith* or you might be calling him *Rob*. Many years ago, almost all children would continue to call the mother's friend Mr. Smith and would not even dare to call him Rob. If the child did so, it would be considered rude or funny. These days, more and more people are comfortable with children calling adults by their first names in such situations. Some people prefer the older way and use the Mr. name. Others like the newer way in which first names are used.

The best thing for Daniel to do when he first meets his mother's new friend is to ask his mother and her friend what name they would like him to use: Mr. Smith or Rob? They might say Mr. Smith. This would be fine at first. However, after Daniel's mother starts living with her friend, it does seem kind of silly for Daniel to continue calling him Mr. Smith. Again, Daniel should ask the adults what name they would now prefer him to use. At that time, they would probably not want him to continue using Mr. Smith. Perhaps all would feel comfortable with Daniel's using the name Rob. Or they might make up a new special name like Robby. Or if Daniel feels very close to Rob and starts feeling as if he is another father to him, he might start using a name like Dad, Pa, Pop, Poppa, or a name that is like one of these such as Daddy Rob or Pappa Rob. The important thing is that all agree on what name should be used and that no one forces anyone to use a name that he or she does not like. This is best done when everyone decides on the name together.

Some people think that it might be a good idea for Daniel to call Mr. Smith *Uncle Rob*. I, personally, do not like that idea. Mr. Smith is not Daniel's uncle and never will be, whether or not Daniel's mother marries him. Therefore, this name can be confusing. It could give people the idea that Daniel's mother is living with her brother. However, there are probably children who feel that their mother's friend is *like* an uncle, not really like a father, is not a stepfather, and so want to use uncle. If that's what everyone wants, then uncle should be used. But everyone should know that it might cause some confusion.

PROBLEMS CHILDREN SOMETIMES HAVE WHEN A PARENT LIVES WITH SOMEONE

Sometimes children living in a home with an unmarried parent and his or her friend have other worries. One problem concerns the other parent. The other parent may get very upset and want to take the children away. This is what happened to Ricky and his sister Sarah. Ricky and Sarah's mother decided to live with her friend Gary. And so Ricky and Sarah moved into Gary's house. Their father was very upset when he heard about this. He had some old-fashioned ideas and thought that it was wrong for his children to be living with their mother and Gary. He told everyone that he was going to go back to court and get the judge to take Ricky and Sarah away from their mother. Ricky and Sarah's father said that their mother was an "unfit mother," that she was no longer a good mother because she was living with a man who was not her husband. Although many people told him that his ideas were old-fashioned and that few people believed that kind of thing anymore, he still kept trying to take the children away from their mother.

This made Ricky and Sarah very worried. They loved their mother very much, even more than they loved their father. Their mother hadn't changed after they had moved in with Gary. Ricky and Sarah found their mother just as warm and loving as she had been before. The whole idea of the fight between their parents made both of them very upset and frightened. Although their mother told them that there was nothing to worry about—that the judges where they lived did not think a woman was an unfit mother just for living with someone—the two children were still quite scared.

One day, their mother told the children that they had an appointment to see a judge who was going to decide where they were going to live. She told the children that they had nothing to worry about as long as they were honest to the judge. She told them that each of them would be talking to the judge alone in a small room called his "chambers." The main thing she told them to do was to tell the judge the truth and to answer his questions honestly. Ricky's mother told them that what they told the judge would be private but that it was very important to tell the judge how they truly felt.

And so Ricky and Sarah went to the court. Each of them was quite scared, but each told the judge the truth. They told the judge that they wanted to stay living with their mother and that she had always been a good mother. They told the judge that she was still tender and loving even though she was now living with Gary. Sarah even cried while she was talking to the judge.

A few days later, the children learned from their mother that the judge had decided the children could still live with their mother even though she wasn't married to Gary. Ricky, Sarah, their mother, and Gary were very happy.

Sometimes the other parent will be very curious about what is going on in the new home. This happens when a divorced parent gets married again, but it may happen even more often when the divorced parent lives with a person to whom he or she is not married. This is what happened to Barbara. Barbara's parents got divorced, and they decided that it would be best for Barbara to live with her father. About a year after the divorce, Barbara's father's friend, Stacey, moved in with them. Barbara's mother became very upset when she heard about this. She got so upset that Barbara's father said that it had turned her into a "wild woman." Every time Barbara visited her mother, she was asked a lot of questions about Stacey. At first, Barbara answered the questions. She thought that this would calm her mother down. But just the opposite happened. The more questions Barbara answered, the more upset her mother became, and the more questions Barbara was asked. Also, Barbara felt like a spy giving out all this information, and this made her feel bad about herself. Barbara talked to her father about this, and he suggested that it might be better if Barbara were not to answer all of her mother's questions.

This advice was very hard for Barbara to follow at first because it made her mother so angry when Barbara refused to answer her questions. But after a while she saw that her father's advice was working and that it was better when her mother was given less information. She also then felt better about herself because she was no longer being a spy or tattletale. If your situation is like Barbara's, it's important to learn from her experience. It's most often best not to answer questions that one parent asks you about the other. It's no good for the parents, and it's no good for the children.

Another concern that children sometimes have when a parent lives with another person is whether or not they will get married. Sometimes the children hope they will get married, and sometimes they hope that they won't. There are two important things to remember in such situations. The first is that the decision must be made by the adults. Adults should not be asking children for their advice about getting married, and adults should not be making the decision to please the children. It is the adults who are getting married to one another, and they alone should be the ones to decide whether or not they will get married. The other thing that is important for children to remember is that the adults have to take time to decide. Marriage is a very important decision, and it should not be rushed. The two people are living together to help them get to know one another better, and this takes time. You should not be pushing anyone to make a quick decision. They must take it slowly, and you must be patient. It is only over time that the adults can be sure that they are making the best decision for themselves.

3
WHEN YOUR PARENT
MARRIES AGAIN

Your parent's decision to marry again can be a wonderful thing for both your parent and you. Once again, there will be two adults living in one home. Your parent will probably be happier than when he or she was single, and you can be happier as well. However, when a parent decides to get married again, there are many new worries that a child may have. These may not only be about the child's parent but about the stepparent. If the stepparent has children, the child may have new friends and playmates, but there may be difficulties with the stepsisters and stepbrothers as well. In this chapter, I will talk about some of the worries children may have when a parent first decides to get married again. In later chapters, I will talk about new situations that can arise after the people have been living together for a while. For each of the problems that I discuss, I will suggest ways that help you solve that problem. Getting information and talking about a problem can certainly help. But *doing* something about it is a far better way of dealing with it.

A PARENT'S GETTING MARRIED AGAIN
IS NOT YOUR DECISION

Just as it was your parents' decision to divorce and not yours, it is a parent's decision to get married again. Some children think that a parent should ask a child's permission before getting married. I do not agree with them. In my opinion, a parent should ask children *what they think* and *how they feel* about the plans to get married again, but the final decision is your parent's and the person your parent wishes to marry. By talking about your thoughts and feelings about the new marriage with your parent, you may learn why they want to get married, and it may change some wrong ideas you had. You might then feel better about the new marriage.

There are certain things in life that we can control and certain things that we cannot. We cannot control things like sunrise and sunset, rain, lightning, storms, and snowfall. Parents' divorcing and getting married again are also things you cannot control. You can control how you study, play, and behave. The way you do many of these things will help your new family be happy. You can also control things that can make the new family sad. I will talk much more about these things later in this book. The important thing I want to say here is that although your parents' decision to get married is theirs, you have the power to help make the new family a happy or a sad one.

Tom, for example, was very unhappy when he learned from his mother that she was going to marry her friend Larry. Tom was quite happy living alone with his mother. He got a lot of attention from her during the week, and he got a lot of attention from his father on weekends. Yes, Larry seemed to be a nice guy, but Tom still didn't want to live in the same house with him and his mother. Tom had once heard someone say, "Two company, but three's a crowd." He understood th' to mean that two people alone can have a good time together, but when there's three, it gets kind of crowded, and each person may not get as much attention as he or she may want. Tom kept saying to his mother, "Two's company, but three's a crowd. I don't want you to marry Larry." In fact, it almost got to be like a little poem: "Two's company, but three's a crowd. I don't want you to *marry Larry*."

Each time Tom said this to his mother, she asked him for his reasons. Tom had no good reason. He just didn't want to share his mother with anyone. So his mother said, "I'm sorry, Tom. That's not a good reason for me not to get married to Larry. I love him very much, and he likes you a lot as well. I'm sure if you give him a chance, you'll find that he's a very nice person, and you may get to become very fond of one another. I'm going to marry him whether you like it or not. The decision is mine, not yours. You just have to accept the fact that there are certain things that you cannot control, and my marrying is one of them." This made Tom very sad, but he realized that he had no choice. His father worked all day, so he couldn't live with him.

When his mother first got married, Tom decided that he would spend very little time in the house. He was old enough to play outdoors a lot and visit with friends. At least that was something he *could* control. Also, when he did come home, he didn't have to spend time with Larry. He could watch TV instead. That was also something he could control. However, as time passed, he found that it wasn't so bad living with Larry. After a while, he accepted Larry's invitation to play some games together, and they got to be lots of fun. Tom then gradually changed his mind about Larry, and he was then not unhappy that his mother had gotten married again. Although his mother's marrying again was not something that he could control, it turned out to be a good thing, after all.

SOME THINGS THAT CAN HELP YOU
STOP WORRYING SO MUCH

All new things are at least a little frightening. Even grownups are usually fearful of that which is strange and different. A parent's getting married again is one such scary thing. Not only are the two people who are getting married usually frightened, but their children are as well. One of the reasons why new things are scary is that we don't know exactly what's going to happen. One way of becoming less frightened of new things is to ask questions. The more you learn about the thing you're scared of, the less frightened you're likely to be. You may want to know exactly where you'll be living and with whom. You may be wondering whether there will be a change in the times you'll be visiting with the parent who isn't living with you. You'll probably have a lot of questions about your steppar-ent's children (if there are any) and whether they'll be living with you or spending time with you. You may want to get a lot of information about the stepparent: his or her habits, likes, and dislikes. There are hundreds of possible questions you may have. So ask your parents every question you have about how it's going to be after the new marriage. The more questions that get answered, the more information you'll have and the less frightened you'll be.

It's important to remember that as time passes, things usually become less frightening. You can't really know how good or bad a thing will be until you've experienced it, that is, until you have had the chance to really do or see what will happen. And the more time you have spent in the scary situation, the less frightening it will become. So if your parent is getting married again and you'll be living with one or more new people, your fears are bound to lessen with time as you get used to the new situation. Being *told* about how things will be can help you become less scared, but *living* in the new situation and *getting used to it* helps lessen fears even more.

If You Worry That You'll Lose Your Real Parent Some children are scared that a stepparent will take the place of a real parent and that they will never see the real parent again. Fred lived with his divorced mother. One day, she told him that she was going to get married again. His mother went on to tell him that he would have another father, who would be his stepfather. When Fred's mother told him that he would have "another father," she meant that he would soon have *two* fathers, his real, natural father and his stepfather. Fred, however, thought that she meant that he would never see his real father again and that the only father he would have would be his stepfather. That made him very sad. Unfortunately, he didn't say anything to anyone about why he was so unhappy. Finally, he broke down crying and told his mother how unhappy he was over the fact that he would never see his father again. After his mother explained to him what really was going to happen—that he would have *both* his father and a new stepfather—he was no longer sad.

So remember that your real mother and father will always be your parents. Stepparents are *additional* parents. With a stepfather, you have two fathers. With a stepmother, you have two mothers. Both real parents and stepparents can provide you with love, protection, and all the other things parents can give to children. As I mentioned earlier in this book, this was not always true with stepparents. In olden days, a child usually had a stepparent because a real parent had died. In those days, there were usually only two parents left from four original parents because two had died and the remaining parents got married to one another. These days, children who have stepparents most often still have both of their original parents alive as well. So they usually have two real parents and one or even two stepparents—depending on whether one or both of their parents have gotten married again. This is another reason why children today are luckier than children who lived a long time ago.

If You Worry That Your Stepparent Won't Like You
Everybody wants to be liked by everyone else. No one enjoys being disliked or hated. This is not only true for children, but it is also true for a stepparent. Just as you hope your new stepparent will like you, your new stepparent is hoping that you will like him or her. If your stepparent has been married before, he or she knows what it means to lose a loved one. Your new stepparent has lost a husband or wife and has been through much of what you have been through. This person knows the kinds of feelings someone has after a divorce. So your stepparent also wants to be loved and usually fears that he or she may not be.

There are children who have been treated very badly by a natural parent and will fear that the stepparent will treat them in the same way. This does not have to be so. Just because a boy's mother may have treated him badly and then left the family does not mean that his father's new wife will treat him in the same way. Just because a girl's father never showed very much interest in her before her mother asked the father to leave does not mean that the new stepfather will also show no interest in her. I am *not* saying that the stepparent will always treat a child better than a bad or unloving natural parent. I am only saying that *it isn't necessary* that the stepparent will treat you badly if the natural parent did so.

Later in this book, I will talk much more about how to get along better with your stepparent so that there will be a greater chance that you will be liked by him or her. The important thing I want to mention here is that you won't be liked very much if you do nothing or if you do things that get people to dislike you. So if you're afraid of not being liked by a new stepparent, there may be something you can do about it. Doing those things that will make you more likable is the best way to lessen fears of being disliked. In the same way, a stepparent is not going to be liked by you by doing nothing or by being mean. The stepparent also must do things to get you to like him or her.

If You Worry That Your Parent No Longer Loves You

Some children fear that a parent is getting married again because they have not been good and lovable enough. Sally and her brother Tim lived with their divorced mother. One of the things that the children enjoyed doing most was to climb into their mother's bed in the morning and cuddle, wrestle, and play games. They would jump around and giggle and tickle one another. It was great fun. The two children also used to look forward to evenings when their mother would read them bedtime stories. Then their mother would give them milk and cookies and sing them songs to help them go to sleep.

Then Sally and Tim's mother met a man named Robert. Soon she started seeing Robert very often. One day, their mother told the children that she was going to marry Robert and that they would all be living together. Sally thought, *If she really loved me, she wouldn't need anyone else to love. If I was lovable enough, she'd love me so much she wouldn't have to love anyone else.* Sally didn't realize that you can love more than one person at a time. She also didn't understand that the love of a

47

parent for a stepparent and of a husband and wife for one another is different from the kind of love that a parent has for a child. The grownup kind of love does not have to take away from the love that a parent has for a child. A parent's marrying a stepparent does not mean that the parent loves the children any less or that the children are not lovable. It only means that the parent wants to have more than just one kind of loving relationship.

Sometimes children may not be afraid that the parent *now* has no love for them but that, *after* the new marriage, the real parent will stop loving them and only love the stepparent. As I have said, a parent can love both a new husband or wife *and* a child. It's not a choice of one or the other.

If You Worry That the New Marriage Will Break Up

Children who live in families in which the parents are getting along well do not usually worry about their parents getting divorced. Of course, if parents fight a lot or talk a lot about getting divorced, then children will become frightened that it will happen. But when there has been a divorce and then a parent decides to get married again, sometimes the children get scared about the new marriage. They may fear that it also will break up. They may become frightened about the new marriage breaking up even before the marriage takes place. Because their parents divorced once before, they are scared that it will happen again.

Now I cannot say to anyone, child or adult, that a new marriage will be a good one and that there is no chance that it will end in divorce. Parents who are getting married again usually try to be extra careful about a new marriage. Because they suffered so much pain over the divorce, they usually try very hard to be sure that the new marriage will be a good one. That's one of the reasons why many people today live together before they get married. They want to get used to each other slowly before they make a final decision about whether they will marry one another. This can make it less likely that the new marriage will break up.

There are children who decide, sometimes even before the new marriage takes place, that they are going to do everything possible to break it up. If they work hard at it, they might even be able to make this happen. Now I am not saying that the breakup of the new marriage in such cases is entirely due to the children. I am only saying that the children's trying to break up the marriage is *one* of the causes. If, for example, the children continually give the stepparent a hard time, are always fighting with him or her, and never cooperate and try to be nice, they can make life so miserable for the stepparent that he or she may actually decide to leave. Children who do this sometimes forget how lonely they were before the new marriage. Then, if the stepparent leaves, they are sorry for what they have done because they are once again lonely. So if you are scared the new marriage might break up, remember that if you are nice to your new stepparent and try to have a friendly relationship with him or her, it is less likely that your parent will get divorced again. So you can do your part to lessen your fears that the new marriage will break up.

If You Still Wish Your Real Parents Would Marry Again

After a divorce, many children keep hoping that their parents will get together again. Most children stop hoping for this after a while and learn to accept the fact that their parents are not going to get married to one another again. However, there are some children who keep hoping for many months, and even years, that their parents will marry again. Even though both parents tell such children that it will never happen, they still keep on hoping.

Often, a divorced parent's marriage to a new person finally puts a stop to a child's wishing for a remarriage. Now that a parent is married to a stepparent, there would have to be another divorce before the original parents could get married again. This makes it all the more difficult and all the more unlikely that the original parents will marry each other again.

Unfortunately, some children still keep wishing that the original parents would get married again even after a parent marries someone else. Tom was a boy like this. After his mother and father got divorced, he kept hoping that his parents would get together again. His mother married a man named Bob, but Tom did not stop hoping that his parents would get married again. One day, Tom said to his mother, "Why don't you divorce Bob and marry Daddy again? You divorced Daddy and married Bob. So why don't you just divorce Bob and marry Daddy once more?" The way Tom saw it, getting divorced and getting married were easy things to do. This is not so. Most people take a long time to decide whether they are going to get married or divorced. Most people give a lot of thought to such decisions. But Tom thought it was as easy as changing clothes. Divorcing one husband and marrying another was to him like taking off one coat and putting on another. It's just not that way. When Tom came to understand this, he began to accept the fact that his mother planned to stay married to Bob and not get married again to his father. He gradually got used to the idea and was then less sad. In fact, he found that his stepfather was a very loving and giving person, and this helped him stop all this wishing for another divorce and marriage.

Some children like Tom don't accept the fact that their parents plan to stay married to their new stepparents. They may even try to break up the new marriage by being cruel to the stepparent. As I have said before, this sometimes works. However, the child who does this is usually making a big mistake. He may be losing out on the chance of having a stepparent who could be kind and loving, who could also be a lot of fun to be with.

HOW YOUR PARENT'S NEW MARRIAGE CAN HELP MAKE YOU HAPPIER

Most people agree that the best kind of family for a child is one in which there is a mother and a father, both of whom love one another as well as the children. If the mother and father do stay together even though they are fighting a lot, the children are going to be unhappy. A child who lives in a home with only one parent is not, in my opinion, likely to be as happy as one who lives with two parents who get along well. Children who live with only one parent often hope that they could live with two parents who love each other. A stepfamily offers children a chance to have a two-parent home, which, most people agree, is the best kind of a home for a child to have.

After a divorce, many parents are often very sad. They are often very lonely, as well. Many are angry and miserable. When parents feel this way, they are not as likely to give their children as much attention and love as they would if they were happier. So the children can become sad and unhappy, as well. When a parent meets a new person and likes or loves that new person very much, that parent is going to be much happier. That parent will also then be a better parent to the children. Even though the parent is spending some time with the new person and even though the parent may be spending somewhat less time with the children, the children will usually be happier. They will be happier because the parent is happier. More important than the amount of time a parent spends with you is the feelings they have when they are with you. Their happiness becomes your happiness. So this is another way in which a parent's marrying again can make a child happier.

Stepparents, like most people, usually have relatives. These new relatives can also help children be happier and enjoy life more. If your stepparent is young, it is likely that one or both of his or her parents are still alive. They are your *stepgrandparents* and can be wonderful people to know. Sometimes they give their stepgrandchildren as much love and affection as their

own, natural grandchildren. This is another way that remarriage can help make a child's life happier.

I hope you can see then that there are many ways in which a child's life can be happier when a parent gets married again. I hope you can see also that it is up to you to decide whether you are going to allow these things to help make you happier.

4
THE IMPORTANT SUBJECT OF NAMES

WHAT SHOULD YOU CALL YOUR STEPPARENT?

One of the first questions that must be answered in the new family is what you are going to call your stepparent. This is something that you, your natural parent, and your stepparent should decide together. The first thing to remember is that it's the real feelings that are most important, not what name you use. The second thing to remember is that people should not force one another to use a name they don't like. Also, you do not have to decide on one name that you will always use. It may be that you are comfortable with one name at the beginning. As time goes on, you may find that you prefer using another name. It's reasonable for a child to say, "Right now, I want to call you by this name. Perhaps there may come a time when I'll want to use another name."

Most children call their mothers "Ma," "Mom," "Mommy," or "Mother." Most children call their father "Dad," "Daddy," or "Pa"; others use "Pop," "Poppy," or "Father." It is very unusual to call a stepmother by the name "Stepmother" or a stepfather by the name "Stepfather." Many years ago a child might say, "Stepmother, may I please have a glass of milk?" or, "Stepfather, would you like to play ball with me?" Most people today would consider this way of talking old-fashioned. Although some children call their mothers by the name "Mother," very few call their stepmothers by the name "Stepmother." And the same is true with regard to calling stepfathers "Stepfather."

Some children will like calling a stepmother "Ma" or "Mom." This is especially true when the child loves the stepparent very much. Others may not wish to use the same name for both a parent and a stepparent. They may not wish to call both their father and stepfather by the name "Dad," but they will probably wish to call their natural father or mother the name they have always used and use another name for their stepparent. They might call their mother "Mom" and their stepmother "Momma." These days, more and more stepchildren are calling their stepparents by their first names. Many stepparents do not object to this, but some do. It is important that you respect the wishes of your stepparent and not use a name that he or she does not like. Just as you would not want that person to call you by a name that you don't like, you should not use a name that your stepparent doesn't like. Some children like to combine the stepparent's first name with their name for their parent. For example, a girl might call her father "Daddy" and her stepfather "Daddy Bob."

You may feel very uncomfortable when you first meet a stepparent. It is reasonable at that time not to want to call your stepparent by the name "Mom" or "Dad" or another name that is special for a parent. But you may not feel comfortable calling your stepparent by his or her first name, either. It can become difficult to decide what to call a new stepparent. Some children try to deal with this problem by not using any names at all. They may not be able to start a conversation until their stepparent notices them. This is true even if they need to ask something simple like "Will you please pass the salt." Just think how much time you might end up spending just standing around! This does not have to happen if you try hard enough to find a name for your stepparent that everyone could be comfortable with. If this is a problem for you, talk to both your natural parent and your stepparent. Do not be afraid to ask for their help. If you talk about how you are feeling about this, they can help you find a name everyone is happy with. If you don't, you may miss out on your stepparent's attention.

Sometimes a stepparent will try to force a child to use a name like "Mom" or "Dad" in order to make it look as if there is a very loving relationship when there isn't. In this case, it is all right to tell the stepparent that you do not feel comfortable using this name but that perhaps one day you may be. This may be hard to say, but if you can, you might be able to stop your stepparent from trying to force you to use a name you are not comfortable with. If there is still a problem after you have spoken about it, you might want to show the stepparent the things I say here about names, love, and force.

WHAT NAMES SHOULD YOU USE
WHEN TALKING ABOUT YOUR STEPPARENT?

The best words to use when talking about your step-parent to someone else are simply stepmother or step-father. As I have said before, there is nothing wrong with these words. I think it's very nice if a child, when speaking to a friend, can say, "My stepmother is a very loving person," or, "My stepfather is a lot of fun to be with." If your stepparent says such things as "I never want you to call me your stepmother" or "I never want to hear you say the word stepfather," try to get him or her to see that there's nothing wrong with the word. Try to help your stepparent see that what is important is how you *feel* toward a person, not what word you use to refer to them. It might help to ask him or her to read what I said about the word stepparent earlier in this book and what I say here. Perhaps then your stepparent will not mind your using the word steppar-ent or will try to get used to it.

Now, what about when you have to use the steppar-ent's particular name when you're talking about him or her to other people? If you can't just say "my step-mother" or "my stepfather," what name do you use? In order to answer this question, we need to discuss what usually happens to people's names when they get married.

When a man gets married, he does not change his name. If his name was Mr. John Smith before, his name is still Mr. John Smith after he gets married. When a woman marries, however, she usually changes her last name to that of her husband. If a woman marries more than once, she usually changes her last name to that of each new husband. For example, a woman named Miss Alice Brady marries a man named Mr. Martin Glasser. Her name then changes to Mrs. Alice Glasser because she now takes on the last name of her new husband. People call her Mrs. Alice Glasser or just Mrs. Glasser. Mr. and Mrs. Glasser then have a boy whom they call Eric. His name is Eric Glasser. Then Mr. and Mrs. Glasser start having a lot of fights and problems. Finally, they decide to get a divorce.

Eric's father, Mr. Martin Glasser, then meets a woman named Miss Carol Adams. They come to love one another very much and get married. Miss Carol Adams then changes her name to Mrs. Carol Glasser. People call her Mrs. Carol Glasser or just Mrs. Glasser. Mrs. Alice Glasser is Eric's mother. Mrs. Carol Glasser is now Eric's stepmother. Both are called Mrs. Glasser.

Eric, however, may not be happy about referring to his stepmother as Mrs. Glasser. He may say, "There is only *one* Mrs. Glasser, and she's my mother." Eric is wrong here. There are *two* Mrs. Glassers, his mother and his stepmother. When Eric needs to give his stepmother's name, he should call her Mrs. Glasser.

WHAT HAPPENS TO YOUR LAST NAME IF YOUR MOTHER MARRIES AGAIN?

I have just described how a woman usually changes her name when she gets married. Sometimes this can cause a problem for children who are living with their mother and stepfather. They still have their father's last name, while their mother, stepsiblings, and half siblings have a different last name: their stepfather's. Some children keep their father's last name, some use their stepfather's last name, and some legally change their last name to their stepfather's. Tommy, Lucy, and John all chose different solutions to the same problem.

Tommy Robinson's parents got divorced, and he lived with his mother. When his mother got married again to a man named Edgar Granger, she became Mrs. Granger. Mr. Granger's two girls lived with him, so now he, Thomas Robinson, was living in a home with four Grangers. He loved his father very much and liked the name Thomas Robinson. He felt a little funny at times, especially when he had to give a long explanation as to why his name was Robinson when everyone else in the house was named Granger. It got even more complicated when his mother and her new husband had two more children, a boy and a girl. These new children became Tommy's half brother and half sister, that is, his half siblings. They, of course, also had the Granger name. Even though there were now six Grangers, Tommy still wanted to keep his father's last name, and he remained Thomas Robinson.

A girl named Lucy Harris was in a situation similar to Tommy's. Her mother married a man named Mr. Frank Scott, who lived with his son and daughter. Lucy felt surrounded by Scotts. She loved her father, Michael Harris, very much and saw him often, but she did not like constantly explaining why her last name was Harris and everyone in her home was named Scott. She solved the problem by having her parents ask her school to let her use the name Lucy Scott even though her original name, Lucy Harris, was written on her permanent records.

Although I do not have very strong feelings on the

subject, I think it would have been better if Lucy were not so uncomfortable having the last name Harris even though the other people with whom she lived had the name Scott. There is really nothing wrong with having a name different from the other members of a step-family. Lucy's father, Michael Harris, was also not too happy about what Lucy had done. He understood that Lucy felt a little embarrassed, at times, about having a different name, but he also felt that there was nothing for her to feel ashamed of. After all, she had done nothing wrong. It's no sin or crime if people get divorced; it's just sad. And it's no sin or crime if the remarriage results in a child's living with others who have a different last name. Still, many children do what Lucy did. I can understand their feelings and do not try to discourage strongly a child who wants to do this. I just think that the better, healthier, and stronger way to handle the situation is to keep your real name and not try to hide it for any reason.

John Craig also lived with his mother and stepfather, who was named Stanley Forster. John's father was not very interested in him. He rarely visited John and did not give any money toward his support. John had a very good relationship with his stepfather and felt that he was more of a father to him than his natural father. One day, Mr. Forster asked John if he would like to be adopted, that is, if he would like to become his son. He would then, of course, have his name changed to John Forster. John called his father and asked him if this would be all right with him. John was not surprised when his father agreed. His father had seen so little of him that he knew that he didn't love him very much, anyway. He knew also that Mr. Forster loved him very much. He did not feel that there was anything wrong with himself. He felt that there was something wrong with his father, Michael Craig, because he was a man who could not love his own son, his own flesh and blood. So lawyers were called, and together they all went before a judge. John walked into the courthouse with the name John Craig and walked out with the name John Forster. He felt good about the change. That's how John handled the problem of having a name different from other people in his family. Later in this book, I will talk more about adoption.

Daniel Fine's mother really hated his father. They fought all the time. Finally they got divorced and Dan continued to live with his mother. Although Dan would have preferred to live with his father, the judge said that he had to live with his mother because his father had to work all day, while his mother had much more time to take care of him. Then his mother married a divorced man named Henry Swanson. Mr. Swanson lived with his two boys, Ben and Artie. Dan and his mother moved into the house where Mr. Swanson and his sons were living. Dan liked Mr. Swanson, and he especially liked Ben and Artie. The three boys felt like brothers. Dan also saw his father at least once a week, and they loved one another very much.

Dan's mother didn't like it when Dan saw his father because she still continued to hate her former husband. But there was nothing she could do about the visits. Dan's mother would often say that Dan reminded her of his father. This was especially true when Dan would do something bad. Then she would say such things as

"You're just like your father, always causing trouble" or "You're going to grow up and be as bad as your father."

One day, Dan's mother told him that she wanted him to stop using the last name Fine and to start using Swanson instead. She knew that neither Dan nor his father would agree to Dan's being adopted by Mr. Swanson. She just thought she'd have Dan use the last name Swanson and that she'd ask the school to use the name Swanson even though Dan's official record would have him down as Daniel Fine. Dan got very angry and said, "I'm not going to do it. You just want to get rid of the name Fine because it reminds you of Daddy. That's tough on you. You just want to make him feel bad by calling me Swanson. I won't let you. If anybody calls me by the name Swanson, I won't answer. I'll just make believe they aren't talking. I'll put my fingers in my ears and won't hear them."

Dan's mother didn't answer. He didn't know whether she would go to the school or not. So he told his father what had happened. His father agreed that his former wife just wanted to change Dan's name in order to make believe that Dan's father didn't exist and to try to hurt him. He also said that Dan's mother wasn't respecting both of their feelings. His father wrote a note to the school saying that he did not want Dan referred to by any other name but Fine, which was his real and only last name. The school wrote back saying that they would only use the name Fine. After that, Daniel never heard anything again about this. He suspected that his mother had gone to school and that the school refused to cooperate with her and call him by a name that neither he nor his father wanted to use. It wasn't that Daniel didn't like Mr. Swanson. He liked him very much. It was just that he loved his natural father more and wanted to keep his father's name.

The examples I have given do not include all the situations possible when a child's mother gets married again and changes her last name. A child, for example, might love both fathers very dearly and want to be part of both families. One way to show this is to use a new last name that is a combination of both the real father's and the stepfather's name. For example, Lucy, the girl I spoke about before, might have solved her problem over which last name to use, Scott or Harris, by using the last name Scott-Harris. Her name would then have been Lucy Scott-Harris. Although this is not commonly done in the United States, it is one possible solution to the problem of which last name to use. It's a solution that may protect everyone from hurt feelings.

5
SOME THINGS YOU SHOULD KNOW ABOUT FEELINGS IN STEPFAMILIES

SOME IMPORTANT THINGS
TO KNOW ABOUT LOVE

Many people think that love is like an electric light, that it can be switched either on or off, that there's either love or no love. Actually, we have different amounts of loving feelings: from none, to a little bit, to a very great amount. Love is more like an electric light that has a dimmer. With the dimmer, you can have different amounts of light. The light can be entirely off, on just a little bit so there is not much light, or on all the way so there is a great big bright light. We all feel different amounts of love for different people. We love some not at all, we love others a little, and we love some a great deal.

It's also important to remember that people are *mixtures* of things we like and love and things we dislike and do not love. Even people we love very much have certain parts that we do not like. Also, there are things in people we dislike, or even hate, that we might ad-

65

mire. The more we get to know a person, the more things we learn about that we might like and the more things we learn about that we might dislike. But it takes time to find out about all these different things. Our feelings about all people that we know well are mixed. I like the words *mixed feelings* because they describe better than words like love and hate what kinds of feelings people have for one another.

Even parents and children have mixed feelings toward one another. Sometimes your parents are filled with great love for you. At other times, they get so angry that they might seem to hate you. And the same is true for you. Sometimes, I am sure, you love your parents very dearly. At other times, you are so angry at them that you feel as if you hate them. Most often, though, it's somewhere in between, and your feelings are mixed.

Carl was a boy who was confused about love. One day, Carl started a fight with his brother. His mother got very angry at him and started screaming at him. Then she sent him to his room. As he sat there alone, he began to cry. He wasn't crying because he was all alone in his room. In fact, he sometimes liked being alone in his room. He was crying because he thought that his mother no longer loved him. He kept saying to himself, "If she could scream at me that way, she can't really love me."

About a half hour later, when Carl's punishment time was up, his mother came to his room. Carl was still crying. "O.K., Carl," said his mother, "you can come out of your room now."

Instead of coming out, Carl just kept crying and said, "If you could be so angry at me and scream at me that way, you really can't love me."

"That's not so," replied Carl's mother. "I still love you very much. When I'm angry at you and scream, it's true that I have less loving feelings at that time. But loving feelings are still there even though I'm angry. And now that your punishment is over and you're being good, the anger is all gone, and there are only loving feelings left."

What his mother had said seemed to make sense to Carl. The more he thought about it, the better he felt. He stopped crying and started to smile. He realized that he had had the wrong idea about love. He realized that people can have mixed feelings, and this made him feel very good. He knew that his mother still loved him even though she was angry. He was glad she had corrected his wrong idea about love.

How Can You Tell If a Stepparent Loves You? Stepparents and stepchildren are not different from anyone else when it comes to the kinds of feelings that they have toward one another. Most often, their feelings are mixed, but they can't know what kinds of feelings they will have for one another until they get to know each other well.

Usually, stepparents want very much to love and be loved by their stepchildren. Often, they are afraid that the stepchildren will not like them. Sometimes stepparents will try very hard to have a loving relationship with a stepchild at the very beginning and scare or "turn off" a stepchild. This is what happened to Ben. When his mother first introduced him to Ralph, before she even got married to him, Ralph picked up Ben and started to smother him with kisses. Ben was disgusted by this and squirmed out of Ralph's arms. Although his mother had spoken to Ben about him, Ralph was still a complete stranger to Ben, and he felt very uncomfortable when Ralph tried to kiss and hug him. Ralph also gave Ben many expensive presents. Although you might think that Ben would have been very happy when Ralph bought him these presents, he wasn't. He felt that Ralph was trying to buy his love, and so the presents made him feel very uncomfortable. Unfortunately, Ben didn't tell anyone, not even his mother or Ralph, how he felt. He just keep all his thoughts and feelings to himself. And so he kept feeling sad about what was going on between himself and Ralph. If he had talked to Ralph and his mother about his feelings, perhaps then Ralph might have taken things more slowly and let time help them become friends.

Many children feel unhappy and scared when they get all this attention and affection coming from someone who is practically a stranger. Hugging, kissing, and giving presents are the parts of love that can be given early. But the *feelings of love*, the most important part of love, must grow over time. People need time to get to know one another and to learn about what is lovable about a person and what is not.

Usually, a stepparent does these things because he or she is afraid the stepchild won't love him or her. The stepparent then tries too hard to win the stepchild's love. Sometimes a stepparent will do all these things to make the child's parent think that he or she really loves the child very much when this is not true. At the beginning, it may be difficult, if not impossible, for you, and even your parent, to tell which is really hap-

pening. You might not be able to tell for sure whether your stepparent is just putting on an act for your parent or if he or she really wants a loving relationship with you. With time, however, it will usually become clear.

Another important thing to remember about love is that the best way to tell whether a person loves you is not what the person *says* about how much he or she loves you but what the person *does*. When a person says that he or she loves you, it may certainly be true, but it may not, because saying something is easy. It's best to *see* what the person is doing if you want to know whether there is real love.

People who love you want to be with you when they can, and they want to help you learn and grow. They enjoy touching, kissing, and holding you, especially if you're still quite young. They get upset when you're sick and will spend a lot of time helping you get better. They get upset if you're in trouble and try hard to help at such times. This doesn't mean that they don't discipline or punish you when that is what you need. But when they must punish you, they try not to be too strict, and the punishments are fair. These are the best ways to tell whether a person loves you, whether it is a parent or a stepparent. I hope you will think about these things when you're trying to decide whether your parent or stepparent loves you.

You Don't Have to Love Your Stepparents Very Much, and They Don't Have to Love You Very Much Many children think they should have strong loving feelings toward their stepparents. They may even have been told by their parents and stepparents that they should have loving feelings. Children who have been told this may feel bad about themselves if they do not have these loving feelings.

I believe that it is better to accept the fact that loving feelings toward a stepparent are nice to have, but they do not necessarily happen. There are children who do not love their real parents very much. So why should all children be expected to love their stepparents? In the same way, it is certainly nice—and even wonderful—if a parent loves you very much, but it doesn't necessarily happen. There are some parents who don't love their own children, their own flesh and blood, very much. And there are even more stepparents who do not love their stepchildren very much, if at all. There are some stepparents who would have liked it better if the new husband or wife had no children at all. They accept the children into the new home because that's the only way they can marry the person they love. These stepparents may never develop much love for the children. There are others, however, who love children very much and are very happy that the new husband or wife already has children. Such stepparents may give the children deep love and affection.

It is likely, at first, that if your stepparents already have children, they are going to love their own children more than they love you. Certainly, at the beginning, stepparents cannot be expected to love new stepchildren as much as their own children. They have known their own children since they were born. They have had many years to develop strong loving feelings. You, at first, are a stranger, and you cannot expect people to love you just as soon as they meet you. As I have said, deep love takes time to grow. Sometimes stepparents do get to love their stepchildren as much as their own, and sometimes they do not. It's nice when it does happen, but don't think that it *has* to happen. If you think that they *should* love you, then you may become very sad and disappointed. Once in a while, a stepparent will come to love a stepchild even *more* than a natural child, but this doesn't happen very often. So I would not suggest that you hope for this. If you do, you may end up very, very sad.

If it makes you feel bad when you see that your stepparent loves his or her children more than you, it can help you feel better when you think about the fact that your natural parent probably loves you more than your stepsiblings. Therefore, all the children are in the same situation. All are usually getting more love from the natural parent and less love from the stepparent. But no one is likely to be getting more or less love than anyone else. No one is getting all that he or she wants, but no one is getting no love at all, either.

Loving feelings between two people grow best when *both* persons try to be nice to one another. Both must work at it and try. Sometimes the loving feelings do not grow because one or both are not trying hard enough. If you are not trying to get along with your stepparent, then that may be the reason why he or she is not very loving toward you. If this is what's happening to you, it may be that if you start being nice and you start cooperating, you may start getting loving feelings from your stepparent.

However, there are stepparents who will not try to be

nice, and that's the reason why their stepchildren don't feel loved by them. The best thing you can do in this situation is to discuss it with your real parents and the stepparent and see if you can solve the problem. Sometimes you will be able to, and sometimes you will not. If you still can't change the situation, you can at least say that you've tried. As I have said before, "Nothing ventured, nothing gained." If you try something and succeed, you'll really feel good about yourself. If you don't succeed, you can at least say that you've tried. But if you don't try at all, there's no way that you can enjoy the pleasures of success.

Gail's situation is a good example of how speaking up helped improve things between a stepparent and a stepchild. Gail lived alone with her mother. One day, her mother met a man named Nat who lived with his son Dave. After they got to know one another quite well, Gail's mother and Nat decided to get married. Gail and her mother then moved into Nat's house. At first, Gail was very excited about the idea. Her father had not been very nice to her, and she hardly ever saw him. Also, she liked Dave, who was one year older than she was. She had never had a brother and had always wanted one. Now she could finally have one.

However, after her mother got married and they were all living together, things were not as much fun as Gail thought they would be. Nat used to spend a lot of time playing ball with Dave and going to his Little League games. He didn't seem to be interested in doing the kinds of things Gail liked to do, things like reading stories and planting flowers in the garden. This made Gail very sad, but she didn't say anything to anyone. She just kept her anger inside and walked around moping a lot. When her mother and Nat asked her what was wrong, she said that she was all right and that nothing was bothering her.

One day, her mother came to her and said, "Gail, I know you've been very sad since Nat and I have been married. I just know that you've got a lot of things on your mind that you're not talking about. I've even heard you crying in your room. I wish you'd tell me what's wrong so I can try to help you. If you don't, the trouble is not likely to go away. If you do, then we can at least try to solve the problem."

Gail suddenly burst out crying. "It's Nat," she screamed. "I hate him. And I hate Dave and all those stupid Little League games. You told me I was going to get a new daddy. He's not a father. He's just a baseball player."

Gail's mother then answered, "I *thought* that it was something like that. I think we should talk to Nat and Dave about this problem and see what we can do. I know this is very painful to you, and it hurts me to see you cry so hard. But I'm glad you've finally told me about it because now we know how to start trying to do something about it."

Gail was relieved. Her mother had not been angry at her for what she had said. In fact, her mother was going to help try to solve the problem. This made her feel even better. She was already glad she had spoken up and told her mother what was wrong.

So the four of them sat down in the living room that evening. It was hard at first, but Gail did tell Nat how bad she felt about all the time he was spending with Dave and how little interest he had in the kinds of things she liked to do. To Gail's surprise, Dave made the same complaint about her mother. It seems that Dave and his father had only learned how to do father-son things and Gail and her mother only mother-daughter things. They all decided that they would try to practice doing father-daughter and mother-son things as well. They made a list of the things they would try. They knew that they would learn to like some of them and not others. After they had all tried doing different things with each other, they were all glad that Gail had finally spoken up. They enjoyed being with one another much more, and the loving feelings between the stepparents and stepchildren got stronger and stronger.

Sometimes there are few, if any, loving feelings between a stepparent and a stepchild, and it's no one's fault. Each has tried, and each has failed. We cannot love everyone, and we cannot be expected to be loved by everyone. There are many different kinds of people in the world. In fact, no two people are exactly the same—even twins. That's one of the reasons why the world is such an interesting place—there are so many different kinds of people. Just because you and your stepparent do not love one another does not mean that there is necessarily anything wrong with either of you. It may just mean that you're different kinds of people. Just because your parent loves your stepparent does not mean that you have to love your stepparent, also. And just because stepparents love their own children does not mean that they have to love you as well. This does not mean, however, that you cannot live together in peace with a stepparent. Even though you don't love a stepparent very much, it does not mean that you shouldn't cooperate and try to get along with him or her. Later on, I will talk more about the things you can do to help you get along better with a stepparent.

SOME IMPORTANT THINGS TO KNOW ABOUT ANGER

There are many things that happen to children of divorce that can make them angry. Most children get angry about the divorce. They don't like the idea of living in a home with only one parent. They don't like all the trouble of having to see one of their parents by appointment during visiting times. There is usually less money available after a divorce, so the children cannot buy as many things as they could before the separation.

When a parent gets married again, there are even more things happening that can make children angry.

76

They may have less time with the newly married parent than they did before. They have to live with more people. Often, it is much more crowded. There is less freedom for the children to do what they want when they want to. More sharing and cooperation are necessary to keep peace in the house. All these things can make children angry. They cause angry thoughts and angry feelings.

Some people have the idea that angry thoughts and feelings are bad to have. They think that it's wrong or even sinful to have angry thoughts and feelings. Actually, it's normal and healthy to feel anger. The reason I say this is that everyone has things happen that can make a person angry. There are always things happening that we don't want to happen. There are always things we want that we cannot have. These are the things that can make us angry, especially when they happen often. The important thing to remember is that it's normal to have angry thoughts and feelings and that there's nothing wrong with a person who has them. The other thing to remember is that it's what a person *does* with the anger that's important—whether a person uses it in a good and helpful way or in a bad or foolish way. Here I will tell you about how you can use your anger in a way that will help you rather than hurt you by causing more trouble.

What to Do About Angry Feelings When something happens to get you angry, it's very important to try to figure out exactly what it is that is causing the anger. Sometimes it's easy to find out what it is, and sometimes it's not. Once you figure out what is making you angry, you must decide what you can do to make you feel less angry. Angry feelings are uncomfortable; you cannot feel happy while you're angry. So it's a good idea to do everything possible to get rid of angry thoughts and angry feelings.

One of the worst things you can do is to keep angry feelings inside and not talk about them. Then they just build up, get worse and worse, and you get angrier and angrier and more and more unhappy. The best thing you can do is to talk about your angry feelings with the people who are making you angry. The purpose here is to solve the problems that are causing the anger. It's best to do this as early as possible, before the anger builds up. When the anger is small, you can talk about it calmly. That's the best way to talk about anger, and that's the way that makes it more likely that you'll be

able to solve the problem. When anger gets too big, people start yelling and having tantrums. Then it's very hard to solve problems.

When you tell people why you are angry, it is a good idea to use words that are more polite than those that may first come into your mind. It is normal for dirty words and curses to come into your mind if you are angry. Although these words do help let out a lot of anger, they usually make others, especially adults, even more upset. It is important that you use the anger to change the things that are getting you angry in the first place. Then you will no longer be angry. Sometimes you can change the thing that is causing the trouble; sometimes you cannot. Whether or not you can change the thing, it's very important to *try*. There is an old saying that is one of the wisest that I know. It is so wise that many people make signs of the saying and hang it on their walls. The saying is: *God grant me the serenity to accept the things I cannot change, courage to change the things I can, and the wisdom to know the difference.*

The saying is almost like a little prayer. It asks God to help a person be calm and serene enough *not* to try changing things that cannot be changed. It also asks for bravery and courage to try changing the things that can be changed. Lastly, it asks for good sense and wisdom to know the difference between those things that can be changed and those things that a person cannot change. I think that this saying is so wise that I show it to my patients, both young and old. When something gets you angry, you have to try to change the things that you can and accept those that are impossible to change. You have to try to tell the difference between those things you can change and those you cannot.

There are some children who think that if they get angry at a stepparent, the stepparent will throw them out of the house. Children do not usually fear that natural parents will do this. They do not usually fear that natural parents will throw a child out into the street for getting angry, having temper tantrums, or calling them names. A stepparent, however, was once a total stranger and even now is not a blood relative. Children usually know that a natural parent would miss them if they were gone, but a stepparent, they feel, would probably not miss them. In fact, they often feel that the stepparent might be glad to get rid of them.

Sometimes it is true that a stepparent would be happier if the stepchildren weren't around the house. This is especially true when the stepchildren cause a lot of trouble, but even then a stepparent cannot throw a child out of the house. Even if a stepparent wanted a child out, he or she could not do it. It's against the law for anyone to throw a child out into the street. Also, the natural parent is there to stop such a thing from happening. So this worry is not something that should keep you from telling your parent and stepparent about how you feel. Remember, if you express your angry feelings early, when you can be polite about it, there will be even less of a chance that you will get your stepparent angry.

Using the Wrong Person as a Target for Your Anger
A common problem that children of divorce have is letting out their anger at the wrong person. Often, the real person who makes the child angry is not the one who gets any of the angry feelings. It is another person who is used like a target and gets most, if not all, of the anger. Often the child is scared to tell the original person about the anger and feels safer letting it out on somebody else. This does not help solve the problem, and it can make it even worse.

Carol was one child who kept getting angry at the wrong person. Her father was not good to either Carol or her mother. He was not interested in his family and did not spend much time at home. One day, he told Carol and her mother that he was leaving. This was no big surprise to anyone because he was hardly around the house anyway. Although Carol was angry at her father for leaving, she was afraid to tell him. She was scared that if she told him how angry she felt, she would see even less of him. After the separation and divorce, Carol only saw him once in a while. He would never say in advance when he would be coming or how long the visits would be. This made Carol even more hurt and angry, but she didn't tell her father because she feared that he might stop visiting entirely.

What Carol did was to let her anger out at her mother. She got angry at her mother for the slightest thing. Carol would call her mother bad names, throw things at her, spit at her, and kick her. Carol's mother was very kind and loving and did not deserve all this bad treatment. No matter how well Carol's mother treated her, Carol would often get angry at her. No matter how badly Carol's father treated her, she was nice to him. If Carol had spoken to her father and told him how angry she was, she might have changed things. If Carol had let out the anger she felt toward her

father—and let it out politely before it got built up—he might have come to visit her more often, and he might have paid more attention to her when he was with her. Because she didn't tell him these things, he did not change. Of course, he might not have changed even if she did tell him. Whether or not letting out her anger would have changed him, it probably would have helped her be less mean to her mother, and Carol would have been able to enjoy her mother more.

Mike was another child who kept getting angry at the wrong person. After his father left, he kept blaming him for everything. Although his mother was often mean, Mike would never show any anger toward her. In fact, it was the mother's meanness that was one of the important reasons that Mike's father left. Although Mike's mother was often mean to him, Mike was scared to let her know how angry she made him. He was scared that if he let her know how angry he was at her, she, like his father, would leave, and then he would be all alone. He kept acting as if his mother could do no wrong and his father could do no right. If Mike had told his mother that it got him angry when she was mean, she might have tried to be nicer, and he might have started to see that his father was not all bad. But since he didn't speak up, nothing changed, and the trouble continued.

Children living in stepfamilies may also take out anger on the wrong person. A child might seem to be angry with a stepparent when he or she is really angry at one of his or her real parents. You may think stepparents are good targets for anger because they aren't as important as real parents and that if they leave, not much is lost. You think that if you lose a parent, you are really in trouble but that your stepparent is not as important. You may feel that since you have lived without your stepparent before, you could live without him or her again. But these could be wrong thoughts.

George was very upset when his father left home, leaving him to live with his mother and sister. George's father hardly ever saw the children. George was scared to tell his father how angry he was at him because he feared that he might then see even less of him. When George's mother married again, there was trouble from the very beginning. George *hated* his stepfather, but there was no good reason for his hatred. His stepfather was a kindly person and wanted very much to like and be liked by George. But George didn't give him a chance. George mostly ranted and raved at his stepfather. Had he spoken politely to his father about the anger he felt, he might have gotten more attention from him, and then there wouldn't have been so much trouble between George and his stepfather.

Now I am *not* saying that letting out anger in a polite way to the person with whom you are really angry will always work and that the person will always change. Sometimes the person will, and sometimes the person won't. If the person doesn't change, then you have to do other things to help make you less angry, things like enjoying yourself with others so that you won't feel so sad and lonely. The main thing I *am* saying is that there is little, if any, chance of changing things if you just let your anger out at the wrong person. That actually makes things worse. It gets you into trouble with the wrong person and doesn't solve any problems you are having with the person you are really angry at.

The Story of King Pyrrhus Over two thousand years ago, in ancient Greece, there lived a king named Pyrrhus. In King Pyrrhus's time, there were many wars, and Pyrrhus led his men into many fierce and bloody battles. It appears that King Pyrrhus spent most of his time fighting various tribes and people who lived in his part of the world. These battles left little money for other things. And nobody knows exactly how many thousands and thousands of men lost their lives in them.

Once King Pyrrhus fought a particularly horrible battle against the Romans at a place called Asculum. Although Pyrrhus won the battle, he lost his most im-

portant officers and most of his men. At the end of the battle, Pyrrhus declared, "One more such victory and I am lost." By this, King Pyrrhus meant that if he were to fight another such battle, even though he might win, he would no longer have an army and could no longer either defend his people or fight against others. Pyrrhus's victory, then, was really a defeat. He had lost much more than he had gained. Since that time, such victories are called *Pyrrhic victories*. When people say that their victory was Pyrrhic, they mean that even though they won the battle or the war, they really lost much more than they gained.

Now you may be wondering what all this has to do with children living in stepfamilies. It may have nothing to do with you, but it has much to do with some children. Unfortunately, some children swear that they will do everything in their power to break up the new marriage. They decide, even before they know their stepparent very well, that they hate him or her. They swear that they will do everything possible to break up the new marriage and get rid of the stepparent. They never give the new stepparent a chance to relax and enjoy good times with them. Instead, they are continually fighting. They may fight for weeks, for months, and even for years without letting up. Unfortunately, it sometimes happens that these children are successful. They make life so miserable for their stepparents that the marriage is broken up. The stepparent who leaves the home might even say, "The marriage might have been a good one, if not for that child. He started making trouble for me the very first day I met him, and he hasn't stopped since. I just can't take it any

longer." He may go on and say to his wife, "I love you still, and I would like very much to live with you. However, I cannot live any longer with that child."

Such a child has won a victory. However, it may have been a Pyrrhic victory. He may have lost much more than he has gained. The stepparent might have been someone with whom he could have had many good times. The stepparent might have given him much love, attention, and affection. The stepparent might have taught him many useful things and given him guidance and protection. Such a child has lost much more than he has gained. Therefore, if you are one of those children who is constantly at war with your stepparent and you hope that you will someday be successful in getting rid of him or her, be sure that you understand what this means. Be sure that you will not

87

lose much more than you will gain. Be sure that you don't end up with a Pyrrhic victory.

Now I am not saying that all stepparents are fine, good, loving people and that children should never be angry about a remarriage. There are times when a stepparent may cause a child great difficulty, and there are even times when a child is better off if the new marriage breaks up. Most often, however, children are better off with new marriages because they once again have a home in which there is a mother and a father.

So if you do feel that you would be better off if your parent and stepparent get a divorce, the best thing to do is to discuss why you feel this way with your parent and stepparent, both alone and together. Try to solve the problems by talking about the things that bother you. Perhaps you will be able to change these things, perhaps not. But at least you will be able to say that you tried. If you can't change certain things, it may be that you will have to put up with them for some time. However, the day will come when you will have grown up, will be out of the home, and will no longer have to put up with these things.

SOME IMPORTANT THINGS
TO KNOW ABOUT LOYALTY

Now I will talk about loyalty. The meaning of the word is not easy to explain. Loyalty is a feeling that we develop toward people we care about. Sometimes it means that we protect someone from somebody else. For example, we would say that a big brother is being *loyal* to his smaller brother when he helps him fight off big bullies. The little brother feels that he can count on or trust his big brother to help him when he is in trouble. Sometimes being loyal to someone means being on their side when they are having trouble. Most children have faith that their parents will help them with problems. Parents also hope that their children will be loyal to them, that the children will take their parents' side when there are problems. Husbands and wives hope that they will be loyal to one another. In a good family, everyone is loyal to everyone else. They trust each other and support each other when someone from outside the family is causing trouble.

The opposite of loyalty is *disloyalty*. When you think that a certain person should take your side, and they don't, you feel that the person is being *disloyal* to you. When you have no trust that you can count on that person to help you when you need it, you feel he or she is a disloyal person.

One of the biggest problems that stepfamilies have is *loyalty fights*. There are different kinds of loyalty fights that happen because some members of the stepfamily feel loyal to two people at the same time. This can be a very difficult problem to solve, and I have given several different examples of how some families handled their loyalty fights to show you how they can happen and how they can be solved.

How a Parent Can Be Caught by Divided Loyalties Jim lived with his father and stepmother. One day, Jim and his stepmother had an argument. Jim's stepmother decided to discuss the whole thing with Jim's father. When Jim's father got home from work, he listened to both Jim's and his wife's side of the story. He found himself, however, caught between his new wife and his son. If he took his wife's side, Jim might feel that his father was being disloyal to him. If he took Jim's side, his wife might feel that her husband was being disloyal to her. Jim might feel that his father didn't love him very much if he took his stepmother's side, and Jim's stepmother might feel that her husband didn't love her very much if he took Jim's side. He feared that if he took his wife's side, Jim might say such things as "Who do you love more, your wife or me?" "Who do you love more, your wife by marriage or your son, *your own flesh and blood*?" He feared that if he took Jim's side, his wife might say, "You have no sense of loyalty to me if you can disagree with me right in front of this child."

The best thing for Jim's father to do in this situation is to say exactly what he thinks about who is right and who is wrong. He should talk only about the argument.

If, for example, he believes that his wife was right this time, he should say so. If Jim then feels that this proves that his father has been disloyal to him and doesn't love him, Jim's father should say something like "Just because I have taken your stepmother's side on this one thing doesn't mean that I don't love you. Just because I am finding fault with one part of you, with *one* thing you did wrong today, does not mean that I do not love you *at all*. Being loyal to you and loving you does not mean that I have to agree with everything you do and say." And Jim's father should say the same thing to his wife if she feels that he is being disloyal to her if he sides with Jim.

Here is another example. Mary and her stepmother had a fight one day. Mary's stepmother decided to discuss the problem with her husband. Before either Mary or her stepmother could tell her side, Mary's father said, "Leave me out of it. I don't want to get involved. I don't want to take sides." I disagree with what Mary's father said here. I think he was afraid they would be angry at him and accuse him of being disloyal. He knew that if he took the side of either Mary or her stepmother, the other person might be angry with him. But I believe that by saying nothing, he was being disloyal to *both* Mary *and* her stepmother. He could have helped settle the argument by listening to both sides. Somebody should have said to him, "You're copping out. You just want to be 'Mr. Good Guy' to everybody. You're afraid to have anyone angry at you. By not doing anything, you're being disloyal to both of us, and you're making both of us angry at you." If somebody said something like this to him, he might then have gotten involved and given his opinion.

One day, David and his stepmother had a fight. In this case, David's father, after thinking about the problem for a little while, slowly explained how he thought that his wife was right. David was sure that his father really agreed with him. He was also sure that his father was afraid to disagree with his stepmother. But he didn't say anything to anyone. He was very angry inside, especially at his father. He just moped and walked around with a sourpuss face all day. His father continued to side with his stepmother. David knew that his father was being disloyal to him, and he had less and less to do with his father.

One day, David's father sat down with him and asked him why he was so sad all the time, why the two of them no longer did fun things together? David broke down and started crying. He told his father how he felt that he was being disloyal to him. He told him that he thought his father was scared of his stepmother and that he didn't respect him very much for being such a coward. David's father was amazed and upset when David said these things, but in his heart he knew that what David was saying was true.

After that, David's father thought a long time about the things that David had told him. He realized that he had been disloyal to David and that he was scared of making his new wife angry at him. Gradually, David's father changed. He started to say exactly what he felt and sided with the person with whom he truly agreed regardless of whether the person was a child or adult. Although his wife did get angry at David's father when

he sided with David, she gradually came to see that she was in the wrong at times and came to respect her husband's opinion much more. David also came to respect his father much more and no longer distrusted him. After that, they had many more fun times together. David was glad that he had spoken up and said what was on his mind.

Susan lived with her mother and stepfather, Stan. Whenever there was an argument between Susan and her stepfather, her mother took her stepfather's side. Susan knew that she couldn't always be wrong. She just knew also that there were times that her mother really was on her side but was agreeing with her stepfather so that there wouldn't be a fight. She felt that her mother was afraid of her stepfather and so always took his side.

One day, Susan heard her mother and Stan talking.

They didn't know she could hear what they were saying. Her mother was telling her stepfather that she had really agreed with Susan in that last argument. Her stepfather said that it was important that they not express differences of opinion in front of the children.

This made Susan very angry. She charged into the room and said, "Mommy, you're a liar, and I hate you. You've been very mean to me. You never take my side. I know you can't always agree with Stan. What's so terrible if you have a different opinion? If you both have the same opinion all the time, then you must be liars!"

Susan's mother was upset to hear all these things, but she was also ashamed of herself. She had to admit that what Susan had said was true. She realized that no two people can always agree on everything and that she and her husband were not providing good examples for Susan. She began to side with Susan when she agreed with her and with her husband when she agreed with him. Her husband, at first, did not like this new arrangement, but there was nothing he could do about it. After a while, however, he agreed that it was a good idea. Everyone was now being more open and honest, and they then got along much better. Susan was glad that she had spoken up.

Sometimes a child will purposely start a fight with a stepparent in order to see whose side the parent will take. This is a very bad idea. It not only causes extra fights, but it is not a very good way to find out if a parent loves you. As I have said, a parent's taking a stepparent's side in one argument does not mean that the parent doesn't love the child.

It is very important to remember that your parent does not have to make a choice between you and your stepparent. A parent can love *both* a child *and* a husband or wife. It doesn't have to be a choice between one and the other. If you decide that your parent doesn't love you because he or she loves your stepparent as well, then you will be very angry, and you may cause all kinds of trouble with your anger and lose out on a lot of love and fun.

How You Can Be Caught by Divided Loyalties Another common loyalty problem in stepfamilies is that of loyalty fights between parents and stepparents. Here the child is in the middle of a battle to see whom he or she loves more—the mother or stepmother, the father or stepfather. Sometimes a parent or stepparent causes the loy-

alty fight. At other times, there is no conflict between the parents and stepparents. It is the child who believes there is a loyalty fight when there is not.

Your father, if he loves you very much, is likely to be jealous of your stepfather. Whether you live with your stepfather or just visit him, when you are with your stepfather, you are not with your father. This may make your father feel very lonely. He may miss you very much and be jealous of your stepfather, who can be with you when he cannot. If you come to love your stepfather, your father may feel even worse.

There are some children who feel bad about themselves if they love their stepfather. They may feel disloyal to their father because they know that it makes him feel bad that they love their stepfather, too. Such children should realize that there is nothing wrong with loving both men. Since both men love them and want to be with them, it is reasonable that they should love their father and come to love their stepfather as well. There is nothing to feel guilty about. There is nothing to feel disloyal about. Many fathers feel bad when their children love their stepfathers, but they realize, as well, that it is good for them to have a warm, loving relationship with him. So they have mixed feelings about their children's relationship with their stepfather. They don't like it because they are jealous of the time and fun he has with their children. However, they do like it because they know it is good for the children to have such good times.

There are some fathers, however, who are so jealous of their children's stepfather that they try to get the children to dislike and even hate him. They want their children to dislike him so that they won't enjoy themselves with him and will want to spend more time with their fathers. Such fathers, instead of doing nice things with their children in order to win their love, will spend a lot of time saying bad things about the stepfather. There are also stepfathers who will say bad things about the children's father in order to get them to dislike their father and like their stepfather more.

If you are in a situation like this, remember that you can like *both* your father and your stepfather. It doesn't have to be a choice. Do not believe anyone who says that you have to make a choice between your father and stepfather. You don't. As I have said before about love, you can like certain things in each that are likable and dislike things in each that you do not like. Each person is a mixture. The more likable things there are in each, the more you will like and even love each. And it is certainly possible to love many things in both.

In the same way, there are mothers who are very jealous of stepmothers. In fact, it is more common for mothers to be jealous of stepmothers than for fathers to be jealous of stepfathers. The main reason for this, I think, is that for many mothers their children are the only important interests they have. The fathers have both the children and their work to involve them. But many mothers feel empty and lost when they do not have their children to care for. Fathers still have their work to give them pleasure when the children are with their stepfather. Mothers may have little to do when children are with their stepmother. Because of this, mothers, more than fathers, are likely to make their children feel guilty about loving their stepmother or wanting to be with her.

Hank and Susan lived with their mother, who did not marry again. Their father did get married again. When the children visited their father and stepmother, their mother would get very angry because she was then left all alone. Sometimes their mother would say to them things like "Are you sure you want to visit this weekend?" or "You don't really want to go there again, do you?" Actually, the children did like visiting their father and his new wife Penny, who was very nice to them. However, no matter how nice Penny was, their mother was always finding fault with her. Finally, the children found it wiser not to praise Penny to their mother, but she still made them feel guilty about loving Penny. I think that this was a sad situation. Hank and Susan had no reason to feel guilty. They were doing nothing wrong. All they were doing was loving two people, their mother and their stepmother.

One day, they spoke with their father about the problem. It had been bothering them for a long time, but they had not spoken about it. Their father not only spoke to their mother but also suggested that the children speak to her. After a number of long discussions, their mother realized that what she had been doing was bad for the children. She came to realize also that it was good for the children to have Penny's love and attention when they visited. She also realized that there was more to her life than her children and that if she got involved with other things, like work and being with other people, she would not be so lonely when the children left and would not be so jealous of Penny. It took her a long time to change her mind and to do these things, but she slowly did. The children were glad that they had spoken up because their mother stopped trying to make them feel guilty about loving Penny.

Gloria was in a similar situation. Her mother did not get married again and was very jealous of her father's new wife, Pat. Even though Gloria's father and Gloria herself talked to her mother and told her about what I have said here—about mothers making children feel guilty over loving stepmothers—her mother was still jealous of Pat. Whenever Gloria would leave the house to visit with her father and Pat, her mother would still say things like "How can you leave your poor mother alone for the whole weekend? How can you do this to your mother, who loves you so much?" Although at first these things made Gloria feel very guilty, with the help of her father, she gradually came to realize that her mother had a problem. She began to understand that her mother was too involved with her and not involved enough with other people and things. Although it took time, she gradually felt less and less guilty and more and more free to love both her mother and Pat. Her mother, unfortunately, did not change. Gloria felt sad for her mother, but this didn't stop her from visiting and loving Pat.

6
HOW TO GET ALONG BETTER WITH YOUR STEPPARENT

Whether you visit or live with a stepparent, your life is going to change. This is because your stepparent is a new member of your family who does things differently from your parents. Everyone in the family will have to go through a time of getting used to each other, and this new situation can be both exciting and frightening at the same time. Because so many things will be new, learning to get along with your new stepparent can be compared to finding your way in a forest. If a person has a map that shows all the trails, mountains, and other important places and a compass to help find the correct direction, then the way out can usually be found. In this chapter, I will give you some information that will be like the map and compass. I hope it will help you find your way in your new stepfamily.

"WHEN IN ROME, DO AS THE ROMANS DO"
You have probably heard the old saying "When in Rome, do as the Romans do." If you understand what it means, it can help you have a better relationship with your new stepparent.

Rome is a very old and famous city, over twenty-five hundred years old. At one time, it was the center of an empire, and many people from different lands visited there. They often had different customs from the Romans, but the Romans were the rulers. Because no one wanted to be in trouble with the rulers, the visitors told one another, "When in Rome, do as the Romans do." They did not give up their own customs, but when they were in Rome, they followed Roman customs.

This is still good advice. If you follow the rules of the place you are visiting, you will have a better chance of getting along with the people there. People's rules and habits are important to them, and if a visitor is always criticizing, it makes everyone uncomfortable. If you try to follow your hosts' rules, they will probably appreciate it and will probably try harder to get to know you and what you like. Of course, you hope that your visitors will follow this advice when they visit you. It's a good idea for them to try to do things the way you do and to follow the rules of your house when they visit you.

This advice is especially useful when you visit your stepfamily. No two homes are exactly the same. In fact, no two people are exactly the same. Even twin brothers and sisters do not do everything the same way or have the exact same opinions on every subject. And every family is different. People like different foods, clothes, games, books, and just about anything else you can think of. And each home has rules that the people in the house follow. This does not necessarily mean that one home is *better* than the other; they are just differ-

ent. Being *different* is not necessarily the same as being *better* or *worse*.

So when you visit your stepfamily home, the people living there are not going to be doing everything just the way you do at your house. If you want to get along with them, it's useful to learn how they get things done at their house and to try to do them the same way while you are visiting. There may be different bedtimes than you have at home. Their table manners may be different. They may have different rules about raiding the refrigerator or eating between meals. They may have different times when people take baths and showers. Some parents are neater than others. Some allow more sloppiness.

Also, everybody gets nervous or fussy about certain things and not about others. For example, some people don't mind loud stereo music; others do. In some homes, there's no problem when a child spends a long time on the phone. In others, it may cause a lot of trouble. Some people like to sleep late on weekends and get very upset when they are awakened early. In other homes, people get up early and don't mind when others make noise in the mornings.

Try to remember that the more people there are living together, the more rules they need to get along with one another. Without rules that everyone tries to follow, there's a lot of confusion, and nothing gets accomplished. So try to follow the rules and practices of that house, even though they may be different from the ones followed in your house. If you do this, it's more likely that they'll like you. If you don't, there may be a lot of trouble. If you demand that they do things just the way *you* like to, you may find that there'll be a lot of fighting and unhappiness.

Now I am *not* saying that you should do everything just the way they do things. It's certainly important to tell others *politely* if you have a different opinion about something. It's important to try to find solutions to problems by talking about your differences. I *am* saying that when you are visiting your stepparent's home, it's a good idea to try to do most of the things their way, especially daily family routines. And, of course, when your stepparent or stepsiblings visit your house, it's a good idea for them to follow this same advice. In fact, you might even show them this part of the book. Tell them that when you visited their home, you tried to do things their way. When they're in your home, they should try to do things the way they are done in your house. In short, it's good for everyone to follow the old advice. *When in Rome, do as the Romans do.*

HOW TO CHANGE THINGS IN YOUR STEPFAMILY HOME

Even when you try to understand all the rules, there may be some things that you really don't like, things that you want to change. The best way to get things changed is to speak up. As I have said before, it's best to speak up very early, when you first start feeling angry. Ask for a change while you can talk calmly about how you feel, before the anger builds up and you're out of control. If you demand a change while you are having a temper tantrum, you are less likely to get it. When you are speaking quietly and politely,

before the anger builds up, people are more likely to listen to you and try to change the things you want them to change.

One good way for stepfamilies to change is to have meetings where everyone has a chance to talk about family problems. Some families do this once a week at a particular time. Others only do it for special problems. In either case, the meetings help people discuss their differences in a calm way, when no one is so angry that he or she can't think straight. In a family that has these meetings, people who are having an argument that they cannot settle themselves will sometimes decide to wait until the family meeting takes place in order to discuss it with the others. This can be a very good way to settle an argument.

If your stepfamily doesn't have such meetings, I suggest you ask everyone to start them. Family meetings not only help settle problems but also help bring people closer together. Talking about problems and trying together to solve them helps people become friendlier toward one another. It helps them feel that they are all part of *one* family group, and this is a very good feeling to have.

HOW YOU CAN FEEL CLOSER TO YOUR STEPFAMILY

The more people there are in your stepfamily the more rules there will probably be, and the harder it may be to follow them. But remember also that the more people there are, the more chances you will have for loving relationships, the more chances for friendships and fun. So something is to be gained by following the rules even though you may not want to at times. The more you follow the rules, the smoother things will be in the family, and the more love, attention, and friendships you will have.

Another way to feel closer to your stepfamily is to work along with the others on family jobs, chores, and projects. Although some of these may not be so pleasant, they can give you a sense of pride and accomplishment. "A job well done" makes you feel good about yourself. It also makes others happy that they can depend on you to do the job. Also, when people work together on the same job and do it well, they feel that they have all been a part of its success. This makes them all feel closer to one another.

Working together with the members of your family can give you the same kind of good feeling you have

when you are part of a team. When a baseball team wins a game, everybody feels very good, especially when they have worked hard to play well. They feel good because they have cooperated to get the job done well. I hope that you can have these same good feelings with the members of your stepfamily.

WHY MONEY SEEMS SO IMPORTANT IN STEPFAMILIES

Unless a family is very rich, divorce causes money problems. Since most people are not rich, most divorced families have money problems. This is not surprising when you think about the new expenses that families have when there's a divorce. Instead of the people living in one home, they now live in two. Extra clothes, toys, and food have to be bought so that there can be things for the children in each of the homes. Extra furniture, like beds and dressers, have to be bought so that the children will have a place for themselves in each household.

Some parents also spend a lot of money on lawyers in order to get the divorce. This is especially true if the parents are fighting a lot. Sometimes the payments to lawyers go on for years because the two people cannot agree. One thing they often fight about is the amount of money each person should be spending. A father may feel that he is paying his former wife too much money. But she may feel that she is getting too little money. And both become even poorer when they give a lot of money to lawyers to try to solve this problem.

When there is a remarriage, it's not likely that the two new families will have the same amount of money

107

to spend. There is usually a difference, sometimes a big one. A boy may live with his mother in a large house because his stepfather has a good business. But his father may live in a small apartment because he doesn't earn as much money. If you are in a situation like this, you will get along much better with your father if you understand that he doesn't have as much money as your stepfather, and if you don't ask him to buy expensive things or to go places that cost a lot of money.

In some families, a father may earn a lot of money but still not give the mother and children very much after the divorce. This is usually not fair, but the father may get away with it anyway. Then there are mothers who manage to get more than their fair share of money from the fathers. This causes differences in the two homes. If this sounds like your family, try not to ask the poorer parent to spend more than he or she can afford. If you do you'll just cause more trouble and fighting.

Stepfamilies also have money troubles. Take Tammy's situation, for example. Her mother and stepfather, Walter, were always complaining about how little money they had. Walter not only had to pay money for Tammy and her mother, but he also had to give money to his first wife and his two sons, who lived with her. When the boys visited Walter, Tammy, and her mother on weekends, he had to pay for their entertainment as well. This left Walter with hardly any money left over. When she was younger, Tammy got upset when her mother and Walter complained about money. She would get angry at them when they would say, "We can't afford it." In fact, it got so bad that every time she heard someone say, "We can't afford it," she would get mad. Then as she got older, she realized how hard things were for Walter and her mother, and she became more sympathetic. She stopped asking for so many things and accepted the fact that she would have to do with fewer toys and vacations. This didn't mean that no money at all was spent on her, just less than she would have liked. When she accepted this, she was less angry and more happy.

So my best advice to you about money is this: Understand that your family, like most of the families in the world, has less money than it would like to have. If you demand things that your family can't afford, you'll only cause trouble. If you accept the fact that you can't have all you want, then you'll be happier. Most of all, remember that what makes people happy together is not the amount of money they spend on one another, but how much they love each other and how nice they are to one another. There are many poor children who are happy with their parents and stepparents, and there are many rich children who have miserable family lives. Although money helps a little bit, it's love, not money, that is the really important thing.

WHY SOME STEPFAMILIES ARE CONFUSED ABOUT DISCIPLINE

There are some children who believe that stepparents should not punish their stepchildren. Carl was one of them. One day, Carl did a number of bad things. His stepfather explained to him what he had done wrong and told him that he was going to be punished in order to help him remember not to do these things

again. Carl got very upset and screamed, "You can't punish me. You're not my real father. Only my real father can punish me."

Carl's stepfather replied, "Yes, you're right. I'm not your real father. I'm your stepfather. But that doesn't mean I can't punish you. I am a kind of father to you. I have taken on the responsibility to take care of you and to help you grow up to be a good person. That not only means teaching, guiding, and protecting you. It also means doing all the other things fathers do for their children. It means praising and rewarding you when you do good things and punishing you when you do bad things. That's also part of being your father and taking care of you. Now go to your room immediately!"

I agree completely with what Carl's stepfather said. Just as it is part of your stepfather's job to provide you with praise, guidance, and protection, it is also part of his job to punish you. A stepfather who does not punish at the proper time is not a good stepfather. He is not helping his stepchildren to learn right from wrong. This is not only true when stepchildren live with their stepfather but also when they only visit. As long as they are in the stepfather's house, he should help them learn right from wrong. Sometimes praise will do this. Sometimes talking alone will do this. At other times, however, some punishment may be necessary to help children learn these things.

Most mothers agree with me that stepfathers should punish their children. However, there are some who do not. A mother who believes this might say to her husband, "Don't you ever punish that child," or, "If you ever lay a hand on this child, I'll leave you." I believe that these mothers are making a mistake. They are protecting their children too much. They are not helping their children learn right from wrong. Also, they are causing trouble in their marriage by siding with their children against their husband no matter who is right or who is wrong. As I said before, this is a bad idea. A mother should side with the person who is right, regardless of whether it is her child or her husband.

Some children know deep down that their stepfathers ought to punish them. But they still try to get out of being punished by saying that only their real father can punish them. It's best for them when their stepfathers do not let them get away with this excuse. It's bad for them when he agrees, because then they aren't being helped to learn right from wrong.

What I have just said about stepfathers is also true for stepmothers. There are many children who live with their mothers and visit with their fathers and stepmothers on weekends. They may say to their stepmothers, "You can't punish me. You're not my mother." The stepmother might answer, "Yes, it's true that I'm not your mother. But that doesn't mean that I can't discipline or punish you. When you're in this house, it's my job to teach you right from wrong. It's my job to help you grow up to be a fine young person. And if I have to help you remember the right thing to do by discipline or punishment, I'm going to do it."

It's a bad idea for a stepmother to say things like "Just wait until your father comes home." When she does this, she is agreeing with the child that discipline is not her job— but it is. The child may also start to see his or her own father as the "bad guy" and the stepmother as the "good guy." This is wrong, because, as I have said earlier in this book, all people are a mixture of both good and bad qualities, and parents and stepparents are no exception.

SOME SPECIAL THINGS YOU CAN DO TO GET ALONG BETTER WITH YOUR STEPMOTHER

One of the biggest complaints that stepmothers have is that their stepchildren do not appreciate them. They feel that they try very hard to be nice to their stepchildren, to cook meals for them, to shop for their clothing, and to do all the other things that parents do for their children. Yet they often feel that their stepchil-

112

dren do not appreciate all their efforts and, most of all, don't even say thank you.

Charlie, Helen, and Roger were having a lot of trouble with their stepmother, Marie. One day, in a family discussion, their stepmother started crying and angrily said, "I just can't stand it anymore with you kids. I work so hard and get no appreciation. I spend hours cooking the things you like. You come storming into the kitchen like a pack of animals. You gobble up the food like you haven't eaten for a month. Then you race out of the kitchen, leaving a mess all over the place. And worst of all, you never once say thank you. You wouldn't treat a maid that way. I feel that all I am to you is a slave—a slave that you treat like dirt."

The children felt very guilty. They spoke about how they had never said thank you to their mother. They

had never thought too much about appreciating the things she had done for them—the same things their stepmother did. They thought that mothers were *supposed* to do these things.

Their father did not quite agree with them, and he said, "Marie certainly shouldn't be expecting you to act like guests, but she is entitled to be treated with respect and appreciation for her efforts. She has a right to feel angry, and you kids should be ashamed of how little appreciation you have for all the things she does for you. It wouldn't kill you to think about what she does for you and to thank her once in a while. I'm not suggesting that you say thank you if you don't mean it. I'm only suggesting that you thank her if you really appreciate her efforts."

The children didn't like hearing the things their father had said, but they realized that what he said was true. They had not been treating Marie very well, and she had a right to feel disappointed. After that, they tried to think about what she had done for them, and they became more appreciative of her. They not only said thank you once in a while but, more important, told her exactly how they appreciated what she was doing for them. After that, Marie was much friendlier, and they all got along much better with one another.

Now I'd like to talk about another important subject: Your stepmother's cooking. Some children will say to their stepmother that their mother's cooking is better. This is not a wise thing to say. In fact, it can only cause trouble. Such a comment is likely to hurt your stepmother's feelings very much. And there is no good

reason to hurt anyone's feelings if you can possibly avoid it.

The best thing to do is to tell your stepmother about all the foods you like and about all the foods you don't like. Then she will be less likely to serve you something you don't like. However, she still may, at times, serve something you don't like. Or she may prepare the food differently from the way your mother cooks, and this may cause you to dislike it. If this happens, try to eat what your stepmother cooked for you if you possibly can. I'm not suggesting that you choke on food that you truly hate. I am suggesting that you try to eat it and politely tell her that that particular food is one you don't like very much. I'm not suggesting that you lie or that you say you like a food that you really don't. It is not lying, however, to keep quiet and not say how

115

much you dislike something. It is not lying to keep quiet and not say something that would hurt someone else's feelings.

It is important to remember that many women are sensitive about their cooking. It makes them feel good when someone praises them for preparing a good meal. In fact, if you really enjoy what your stepmother has cooked for you, it is a good idea to tell her. This will make her feel good about herself and will cause her to like you more. On the other hand, if you are too critical of her food and are always complaining about it, she is likely to get hurt and angry, and you will have much more difficulty getting along with her.

If you solve problems with your stepmother, she'll treat you better, and you'll be happier. However, if you're fighting with her a lot, she'll complain about you to your father, and then you'll probably have trouble with him as well. If you get along well with her, she'll say nice things about you to your father, and then he'll be nice to you. If you give your stepmother a hard time, you may be helping to make her into the cruel and mean stepmother that people talk about. However, if you solve problems with her, you'll be doing your part to make her the loving stepmother that can make your life a happier one.

SOME SPECIAL ADVICE FOR BOYS
WITH STEPFATHERS

When parents divorce, most children remain living with their mothers, and their fathers move out of the house. When this happens to a boy, especially if he is the oldest child in the family, a part of him may secretly be happy when his father leaves. Although he is usually very sad that his father is no longer living in the house, another part is happy to see his father go. The reason for this is that he may then feel that he has his mother all to himself. As much as he loves his father, he is also jealous of the fact that his father did things with his mother that he could not. His father slept in the same room with his mother, even in the same bed. His mother and father had secrets together that he did not share. Once in a while, they went off on vacation together, leaving him behind. These things can make a boy jealous of his father, so much so that he is not completely sorry to see him go and live elsewhere.

Once his father is gone, a boy may feel that he is now "man of the house." This is especially true if he is the only child or the oldest of all the children. Although he doesn't earn money, drive a car, and do the other things that men do, he may still feel grown up and special because of the extra time that he now has with his mother and because he may now have her all to himself. The days of sharing her with someone else seem to be over.

Then, one day, a new man comes into his and his mother's life. Once again, there is a person with whom he must share his mother. Once again, it is a man who is bigger than he and can do things with his mother that he cannot. If the man becomes his stepfather and if the boy has to live with him, he may get very angry and upset. He may get so angry that he may do everything possible to try to get rid of his stepfather.

If you feel this way, it may help you to remember a number of things. First, as I have said before, every-

117

body loses in a war—both the winner and the loser. Even for the winner, most wars end up as Pyrrhic victories. Next, it is important to remember that a boy can never have his mother completely to himself. Even when there is not a man living in the house, most mothers are interested in meeting new men. Some mothers meet new men, and others do not, but most would like to. As much as a mother may love her son, she still has a place in her heart for other people, especially a grownup man. A boy will generally feel better when he accepts the fact that he can never have his mother all to himself.

Remember, too, that most people are happier when they are sharing their time with more than one other person. No boy wants to have to spend all his time with only one friend. Most boys prefer to spend some time with one friend, some time with another, and then times with a few friends together. The same thing is true of parents, stepparents and siblings. So if it makes a boy feel bad that his mother is givng time to his stepfather, it doesn't mean that she's giving him no time at all. It just means that she's giving him less time. And no one is stopping him from having good times with others, both within and outside the family. In fact, the more good times he has with others, the less jealous he will feel.

It can also help a jealous boy feel better when he remembers that he will grow up and be able to have a girl all to himself, someone who might be as nice and as pretty as his mother. This can start happening when you become a teenager and can continue for the rest of your life. So if you are a boy in this situation, think

118

seriously about what I have just said. It should make you feel better about your stepfather. Perhaps then you will stop fighting with him and stop trying to get rid of him. Then everybody will be happier.

WHY PARENTS AND STEPPARENTS GO ON VACATION ALONE

Everybody needs a rest at times. Your parents and stepparents are no exception. After you have played hard or studied hard, it's nice to rest. After you have worked hard, you want to rest, too. Although parents and stepparents usually enjoy being with their children, there are times when they get tired. Sometimes they want to rest at home. Sometimes they may want to go out. No one likes to do the same thing over and over. Everyone likes a change. Otherwise, life can become

very monotonous, just doing the same things over and over again.

So it's a good idea for your parent and stepparent to go out at night from time to time alone or off with friends. Just as they do things out of the house with you at times, it's good for them to do things with others. It's also a good idea for them to take vacations from time to time without you. Certainly, it's a lot of fun when children go on vacations with parents and stepparents. But it's also important for both children and parents to take vacations separately from one another. For example, it's good for children to go to camp. It gives them a change of scenery and helps them grow up and get used to being without their parents. And it's good for parents and stepparents to go on vacations alone so that they can also enjoy a change of scenery.

Of course, parents and stepparents do not usually leave children alone when they go away from home, whether for the day or an evening or on vacation. They leave a baby sitter, relative, or older brother or sister to take care of you. If the person they leave you with is someone you don't like, it's important to speak up. It's important to discuss this with your parent and stepparent. Sometimes the problem may be the other person; sometimes it will be you. In either case, it's much more likely that the problem will be solved if you talk about it.

There are some children who think that just because a parent and stepparent leave them to go off on vacation alone, this means they aren't loved. This is a wrong idea. Just because your parent and stepparent want to

take a vacation alone once in a while does not mean that they don't love you. Of course, if they go away alone very often, if you hardly ever see them, then it is certainly possible that they don't care much for you. But this doesn't happen very often. Most parents and stepparents don't want to be away from their children very frequently or for long periods of time. They love their children very much and want to be with them. It's just that they want to be alone once in a while for rest and a change of scenery.

When they come back, they are refreshed. They have had a good time and are likely to be happier with their children than before they left. So even though the children may have been somewhat sad and lonely while the parent and stepparent have been away, they find that when the parents come back, everyone is happier.

When parents are sad, children are sad; when parents are happier, children are happier.

Some children try to stop parents and stepparents from going on vacation. They cry a lot and try to make the parent and stepparent feel guilty about going. It is a very bad idea for parents and stepparents to give up a vacation because their children don't want them to go. They are spoiling the children and depriving themselves of rest and fun, which are important for everyone to have from time to time. Parents and stepparents who give in to their children are likely to be very angry at the child who makes them feel so guilty that they don't go on vacation. Angry parents are less loving than those who aren't angry. A child who insists that the parent and stepparent stay is not gaining very much. Although he or she may have gotten them to stay home, the child doesn't get much love and affection from them because they are so angry.

So my final bit of advice about vacations is this: enjoy yourself on your vacations and let your parent and stepparent enjoy themselves on theirs. Then everyone will be happier living together.

WHAT IF A STEPPARENT DOESN'T LOVE YOU?

If, after everyone tries, a stepparent doesn't love you very much, it isn't the greatest tragedy in the world. It does not mean that no one else can love you. It does not mean that there are no other people for you to love. There are still other people who do and can love you. You may still have two natural parents, both of whom probably love you. There are grandparents, uncles, aunts, and other relatives and friends who love

122

you and with whom you can have good times. There are adults you can meet in many places—adults who can like and love you. There are teachers in school, scoutmasters, camp counselors, directors in recreation centers, and many other adults with whom you can enjoy yourself and to whom you may grow very close. And, of course, there are friends your own age with whom you can have good times and who can help you feel loved. However, as I have said, you have to try to win people's affection, and you have to be good, friendly, and lovable if people are to love you. I am *not* saying that you should always do what other people want you to just so they'll love you. I am *not* saying that you should never tell people that you're angry at them so that they'll like you. I am only saying that the better you treat people and the more you try to get along with them, the greater the chance you will have good friends and the greater the chance people will love you.

HOW TO GET ALONG BETTER WITH YOUR STEPSIBLINGS AND HALF SIBLINGS

GETTING USED TO SIBLINGS IS EASIER
THAN GETTING USED TO STEPSIBLINGS

When Kathy was six and her sister was two, Kathy's mother and father decided to get a divorce. About a year after the divorce, Kathy's mother began seeing a man named Greg. Greg had two sons, who lived with him. When the families got together for visits, there were both good times and bad times. Sometimes the four children played well, but at other times they fought a lot. When they fought too much, the parents would decide that it was time for one family to go home, and then, of course, the fighting stopped.

One day, Kathy's mother told her that she was going to marry Greg and that in a few weeks they would all be moving into Greg's house to live with him and his two boys. Kathy was very upset. She liked Greg, but the idea of living in the same house with his two boys made her very unhappy. She would have been happier if Greg had had no children at all, but if he had to have

124

children, why couldn't they have been girls? Before she knew it, the few weeks were up, and Kathy, her mother, and her sister were living in Greg's house.

It all seemed so strange, and it all happened so fast—much too fast for Kathy. Now when there were fights between the boys and girls, there was no other home to go to. What happened then was that people got punished and sent to their rooms. All at once, there were so many things happening that Kathy couldn't keep up with them all. There were new rules, lots of sharing, all kinds of strange habits, shouting and fussing, and arguments over who could use the bathroom. There was fighting over whose favorite food should be served, when people should be going to sleep, and who should do the different jobs around the house.

Before her little sister was born, Kathy had had time to get used to the idea. She had known for many months that a new baby was coming. She had helped to pick out the baby's crib. She had even helped to pick out her sister's name. But Kathy had not had enough time to get used to her two new stepbrothers. It seemed as if they had just dropped out of the sky one day and would be living with her forever. She felt that her whole life had changed and that she would never be happy again.

In this chapter, I am going to talk about the kinds of problems that stepbrothers and stepsisters have when they all move into the same house. I will also talk about what happens when half siblings are born. I hope that the things I have to say here will be useful to you if you are in a situation like Kathy's.

In all homes, brothers and sisters fight. This is true

125

whether or not parents have been divorced. In homes where the parents have never been divorced, the first child has no brothers or sisters with whom to fight. However, as soon as the second child arrives, there is jealousy. Before the arrival of the new brother or sister, the first child had all of the parents' attention. Now the parents are going to share their love and affection with the new child. This usually makes the first child feel very angry. Sometimes he or she wishes that the new baby had never come to the house, that the new baby would leave or be taken away, or even that the new baby would die. In such cases, the first child doesn't *really* wish that the baby would die. In fact, he or she still has loving feelings for the baby as well. It's just that the jealous feelings are so strong that thoughts of the baby's dying also come into the first child's mind from time to time. And all this anger is perfectly normal.

In some families, the parents have only one child. Then, of course, there is no fighting between siblings. When there are two children, there will be some fighting. In some families, the parents decide to have three, four, or even more children. Each time a new baby arrives, the older children get angrier and angrier. Of course, there are usually loving feelings toward the new baby as well. With each new baby, the parents have less time to spend with each child individually, and this makes the other children jealous and angry. However, in families where the parents have never been divorced, the children have time to get used to the arrival of each new baby before it is born. Over a period of many months while the mother is pregnant, they have time to think about the new baby, to ask questions about it, and

126

to get used to the fact that it will be coming. Its birth, then, is no surprise. The children are not shocked when it is brought home, and this makes it easier for them to adjust to the new baby.

Usually, there is at least a year between the birth of each new baby. During this time, feelings of jealousy generally get less and less as the older children come to see that their parents still love them and give them *some* time, even though it may have been less than they received before. Also, they come to see that their own time spent with the new baby and with younger brothers and sisters can be fun. They also come to see that the time spent with everybody together as a family can also be fun.

All this is not true in stepfamilies. The stepchildren usually get to know one another during the period when their parents are deciding whether or not they wish to live together or get married. However, knowing people and visiting with people are very different from living with them. When the parents start to live together or get married, everybody may move into the same house in one day or over a short period of time. This can be a shocking experience. No one has really had time to get used to living with one another. Everything happens all at once. This is the kind of situation in which there can be lots of trouble. It is the kind of situation in which there can be much more fighting among children than one may find between full brothers and sisters in homes where the parents have never been divorced. But there are things you can do to help avoid and solve some of these problems.

STEPSIBLINGS CAN BE USEFUL
TO ONE ANOTHER

Many children think that stepsiblings are just a lot of pain and bother. All they think about is the extra space they take up, the extra noise they make, the extra sharing required, and the extra time parents give to them. Many children are so busy thinking about these things that they don't realize that good things can also happen when children from two different families live together.

Only children, that is, children who have never had a brother or sister, can now have them for the first time in their lives. Most only children are lonely even though they may not have to share time with one or more brothers or sisters. Most only children wish, at times, for a brother or sister. Now their wish can come true.

But even children who do have siblings can find stepsiblings useful. Unless you have a twin brother or sister, your siblings are not going to be the same age as you are. Therefore, before your stepparent and parent started to live together, there must have been times when you wished that you had a brother or sister exactly your own age. Many children, especially only children, wish that their parents would have a new baby exactly their own age. The new baby, of course, is going to be an infant and so will not be a good playmate for an older child.

When stepsiblings move together into the same home, there may be a child who is much closer to you in age than any of your own brothers or sisters. This person can become a very close friend. You may have more in common with this stepsibling than with any of your full brothers or sisters. It is like having a good friend and classmate sleeping over at your house all of the time. I am sure that many of you who are reading this book are in this happy situation. But some of you may be living with a stepsibling near your own age and have been thinking so much about the troubles of living together that you haven't thought about the good part of living with stepsiblings.

Another advantage of having stepsiblings is that there are more children around with whom you can have fun and play games. Every child has had the experience of not being able to play a certain game because there weren't enough children around. Many indoor games require four players, and many outdoor games require many more. Often the game can't be played because there just aren't enough children around. So the chil-

dren have to play a game that might not be as much fun. With stepsiblings living in the same house, this doesn't happen as often. Also, even if you don't want to play a game with many children, with stepsiblings around, you have more of a choice of people to play with. Your own brother or sister may be too young, or your friends in the neighborhood may not be around. With stepsiblings, there is a greater chance that there will always be someone to play with.

There can be other advantages to having stepsiblings. Take Hank, for example. He was the oldest of three children. Hank, his brother, and his sister lived together with their divorced mother. Hank used to feel good about this at times. It made him feel good to be the oldest. It made him feel good to be the one who could do more things than his younger brother Ernie and his sister Ruth. It made him feel good when his brother or sister would ask him for advice or asked for help with something they couldn't do. It made him feel good to be able to help Ernie and Ruth with homework. When kids picked on his younger brother, Ernie would sometimes say, "I'm going to tell Hank on you." Hank liked protecting Ernie from bigger kids. It made him feel big and strong. However, in spite of all the good feelings Hank had about being the oldest, there were times that he wished he had an older brother or sister himself. He wished there were a kid a little older than himself to go to for advice and protection.

One day, Hank's mother remarried. Luckily for Hank, one of his new stepbrothers was two years older than himself. His name was Victor. They became very close. Sometimes they would play the same games together;

at other times, Victor would play with children his own age. As time passed, Hank came to admire Victor more and more. He looked up to Victor and liked to do things the way Victor did them and to wear the same kinds of clothes Victor wore. Most important, he found that he could ask Victor for advice and protection. Now his wish had come true. He was very happy that his mother had married Victor's father. Even though the house seemed cramped with all the new people living there, Hank didn't mind because he was so happy to have an older brother—for the first time in his whole life.

Another advantage of having stepsiblings is the fun of teamwork. I spoke before about the good feelings you can get when everyone pitches in together to do a job. Like the members of a baseball or basketball team, everyone feels good when they have cooperated to accomplish something. Only children cannot enjoy this kind of thing in their own homes. In a stepfamily with many children, there is more of a chance that children will be able to have this kind of good feeling about themselves and about the other children they live with. When everyone works together to clean the house or do the lawn or do some chores, they can feel good about what they are doing even though the work may be hard. Doing such things also helps people feel closer and friendlier to one another.

I hope I have persuaded you that living with stepsiblings is not all bad. There are many good things that can come from your new family. If you think about them and try to enjoy them, I am sure you will come to agree with me.

THE GOLDEN RULE

As I am sure most of you know, the Bible is one of the greatest books ever written. Even people who are not very religious, and even people who are not religious at all, agree that there are many wise things said in it. The Bible was not written by one person. Many people wrote the things in it, and it took over a thousand years to collect all the stories and sayings that are written in it. In the Bible are some of the wisest words that were said by some of the wisest men and women who ever lived.

The wise men who wrote the Bible often went around teaching people lessons that they thought were very important for them to learn. Many people had great respect for the words these wise men spoke. One of their most famous sayings was: "Whatsoever ye would

that men should do to you do ye even so unto them." Another way of saying the same thing is: "Do unto others as you would have them do unto you." This means that you should treat others in the same way as you would want them to treat you. Everyone likes to be treated kindly by others. No one likes to be treated in a mean and cruel way. This advice reminds us to think about how we are treating others, to think about whether we would like to be treated the same way. If all people did this, we would all be nicer to one another, and it would be a very pleasant world.

Although this advice was given a long time ago, it has been passed down from parents to children, from generation to generation, down the years. It is so wise that it has come to be called the golden rule. Like gold, it is precious. Like gold, it is something to keep and cherish. It is the kind of advice that I give to all my patients, young and old. It is the kind of advice that can be very useful to children living in a stepfamily. If you think of the golden rule often and follow what it says, you will get along much better with your stepsiblings. They will like you more, and they will treat you better. Then everyone will be happier.

SHARING

Sharing is certainly not most children's favorite subject. In fact, I would guess that it is one of the most unpopular subjects that I could bring up. But there are still some things about sharing that can be useful and enjoyable, and I want to talk about them here. Later I will talk about *not sharing*. It may come as a surprise to you, but there are times when I think you should *not*

133

have to share. I am sure that many of you will be especially happy to read that section.

When children move together into a new stepfamily, one of the first things that they have to learn how to do is share. Of course, all children, even children whose parents are not divorced, have to learn how to share. They have to learn to share with their sisters and brothers, and they have to learn to share with their friends. They have to learn to share even if it sometimes makes them feel bad. They have to learn that if they don't share, if they are selfish, others will be angry with them and not want to play with them. In a stepfamily, however, much more sharing is needed for people to get along well. If they don't share, then there will be a lot of fighting.

When children move into a stepfamily home, they sometimes have to share their rooms. You may have had a room all to yourself, and now, for the first time, have to live in the same room with someone else. You probably have had your own closet or dresser. Now you might have to share these and they may become quite crowded. Before, you may even have had your own television set. Now you can't just watch any program you want; you have to consider what the others want to see. (One way to prevent a lot of fighting about TV is to take turns having first choice. One time, one child has first choice of which program to watch; the next time, another child has first choice.)

One of the most important things that children have to share in a stepfamily is the time and attention of their parents and stepparents. The adults cannot give as much time and attention to each child as before.

This does not mean that they give *no* time at all. It just means that they have *less* time for each individual child. It may help to remember the old saying, *Half a loaf is better than none.* This means that if you cannot have a *whole* loaf of bread, it is far better to have *half* a loaf than *no* bread at all. Some children don't realize this. They act as if having half of what they want is as bad as having nothing. They don't realize that having half of what you want is much better than having nothing and can be almost as good as having all of what you want.

Living in a stepfamily can help you learn some good things about sharing. I'm talking now about the good feelings it can give you to make another person happy. One of the greatest pleasures a person can have in life is doing helpful things for others. When you share what you have, it makes the other person feel good.

135

And it also makes *you* feel good yourself as you watch the happy face of the person to whom you have given something. So when you share, two people are rewarded, the giver and the person for whom the good deed was done.

That is what happened to Joan. Her parents were divorced, and she lived with her mother. Both of her parents had good jobs, and although they weren't rich, they each earned a fair amount of money.

Joan had many fine toys. One day, her mother re-married a man named Carl. Carl was a very smart man. He was a professor, that is, he taught in a college, but he didn't earn very much money. Also, he had to give a lot of what he earned to his ex-wife and his little daughter Tara, who lived with her. Because of this, he had very little money left over to buy toys for Tara. Certainly, she had some toys, but not too many, and they certainly weren't the expensive and beautiful ones that Joan's parents could afford to buy her.

When Tara came to Joan's house to visit with her father on weekends, she admired Joan very much. Joan was like a big sister to her and treated her very well. One of the nice things Joan did was to share her dolls and other toys with Tara. This made Tara very happy. It made Joan feel good to see the big smile on Tara's face when she hugged and played with Joan's dolls. Sometimes Tara wanted to play with just the doll that Joan was in the mood to play with. But Joan would let her play with it, anyway, because it made her feel so good to see Tara happy. So both girls got something: Tara got the joy of playing with the dolls, and Joan got

136

the joy that comes from helping make another person happy.

Another good reason for sharing is that if you share your things with others, they are more likely to share their things with you. It may make you feel bad when they are playing with your toys and you are not. But there will be other times when you'll be playing with their toys and they won't be. So sharing may cause you some bad feelings, the feelings of not playing with your own things, but it can also give you good feelings when the other person lets you play with his or her things.

If you don't share, you don't have the bad feelings of not being able to play with your own toys that minute, but you lose out on the good feelings as well. Also, if you don't share, people will think you're selfish and get angry at you. Then there will be a lot of hard feelings and fighting. When people are angry at you, they may

not want to play with you, and you may become very lonely, even in your own house. Nobody likes to be with a selfish person.

Another important thing to remember about sharing is that you may be getting more rather than less when you share. It is true that you now have to share your mother or father with your new stepparent. Because of this, all you might think about is how your parent will be spending less time with you and more time with the new husband or wife. What many children don't realize is that now there will be *two* adults in the house with whom they can spend time. So they may end up with just as much time with grownups as they did before.

This is exactly what happened to Diane and her brother Frank. They were living with their divorced mother and saw their father on weekends. When their mother told them that she was going to marry her friend Pat, the two children were very upset. Pat had two children who were living with him. Soon all six of them would be living together. Now that their mother was going to marry again, Diane and Frank thought that they would see less of her because she would be spending more time with Pat and his children. Well, something happened that made them realize that they didn't have so much to be upset about. They found that Pat was a wonderful person to be with. Even though they liked being with their mother, there were many more things they could do with grownups now that Pat lived with them. They now had two grownups living with them, not just one. Of course, their mother also spent time with their stepsiblings, but they had two new children in the house to play with.

In short, the children lost something because they had to share their mother with their stepfather and his children. They gained something because they were able to have good times with three new people, Pat and his two children. The sharing, then, wasn't all loss. They got things in return as well.

NOT SHARING

In spite of the good things that can happen from sharing, there are times, I believe, that it is better *not* to share. I am sure that many of you are happy to hear me say this. Sharing is fine, but too much of it can cause problems. There are some families in which the parents may say that everything belongs to everybody, that there is no such thing as personal property. The parents may say that because the father and mother buy everything, they have the right to decide who owns what. They may decide that everything brought into the house is owned by everyone and should be shared by everybody.

I do not agree with this. As important as sharing is, it is also important to have the feeling that there are certain things that you own, that there are things that are your personal property, that you can have all to yourself.

One girl I know has a doll that is very dear to her. She takes it to bed with her at night and hugs it as she goes to sleep. She gave it a special name and enjoys making believe that the doll is her little friend. She likes waking up each morning and seeing that it's still there. I do not believe that such a precious possession should be considered the property of everyone in the house. The girl should have the right to say whether or not she wants to lend it to someone.

Erika had a little music box that a good friend of her mother had given her. When she opened the lid, a little ballerina popped up and twirled around. At the same time, the box played a pretty song called "Raindrops." It was hers and only hers. When she played with it, it made her think of the friend who had given it to her. Her mother did not make her share it with anyone. In fact, her mother wouldn't let her take it out of the house because she feared Erika might break or lose it. Erika also had a favorite teddy bear that she cuddled with every night as she went to sleep. This was also all her own, and her mother didn't make her share it with anyone unless she wanted to.

One day, Erika was jumping rope with her friend Janie. Suddenly, Janie tripped on the rope and fell down. She hurt her foot and knee and began to cry. Erika felt sorry for her friend and wanted to help her feel better. She took her favorite teddy bear, the one she went to sleep with each night, and asked Janie if she would like to cuddle with it. She also brought over the music box and opened it up. Erika said to Janie, "Listen to this pretty music. It will make you feel better." That's exactly what happened. As Janie cuddled the teddy bear and watched the ballerina, she felt much better. Erika felt very good too. Then they went back to jumping rope. Erika's teddy bear and music box were all hers. And it was she, and she alone, who decided when she was going to lend them to someone else.

Having your own property helps you feel good about yourself. Having a special place that is all your own can

140

also give you a good feeling. In most stepfamily homes, children have to share rooms. But most children can at least have their own beds. A younger child might want to sleep together with another child from time to time, but everyone knows who is the owner of the bed and who is the guest for the night. Some children have to share their closets. Then, it's usually best for each person to hang his or her clothing in a certain part of the closet. Then you know exactly which part of the closet belongs to you. Some children have to share a dresser. But each child should have a separate drawer that is his or her own, a drawer for private possessions that no one else is allowed into. Everyone needs a sense of privacy. Everyone needs a place to keep secret things, a place where no one else is allowed to look.

The same is true for toys. I believe that each child

141

should know exactly which toys are his or her own and which belong to others. I also believe that each child should have a special place for his or her own toys. It may be a special drawer, a special shelf, a special cubby, or a special corner of the room. As I've said, I think you should be generous with your toys and let others play with them, but it is the owner of the toys who decides who plays with the toys and when. If you want to be kind and generous and let others play with your toys often, then you will have many friends. If you decide you want to share sometimes and not others, that is O.K. If, however, you are mean and choose not to share at all, you are not going to have many friends, and it will be your own fault. But the decision to share should be yours.

WHAT EVERYONE IN THE FAMILY CAN DO TO DECREASE FIGHTING AMONG STEPSIBLINGS

I sometimes hear parents say, "They fight like cats and dogs." Have you ever wondered about this saying? Although cats and dogs can indeed fight, there are many cats and dogs who live together and hardly ever fight. I'm sure you know someone who owns both a cat and a dog, and the two animals hardly ever fight. In fact, the cat and dog may get along very well with one another and be good friends. Children can also live together without fighting all the time. You don't have to fight like cats and dogs if you don't want to. The things I have already told you about sharing can lessen the amount of fighting among stepsiblings. Here are some more things you and your stepsiblings can do.

Understanding Differences One way to keep fights from starting is for each person to remember that what is different is not necessarily bad or wrong. Every home has its own style, its own way of doing things. Your stepsiblings have done things one way in their home, and you have done things another way in yours. This does not mean that one way is better than the other. It just means that people do things differently. They might like certain foods that you may not. You may like certain kinds of music that they hate. Some children like to study more, and it is important to them to be good students. Others are more interested in sports and are happy if they just pass their subjects. Some like to have many friends; others are happy with just a few. Some speak loudly and seem to make a lot of noise wherever they are; others don't speak as much and are quieter. Some eat a lot; others aren't that interested in food. Some talk a lot about clothing; others couldn't care less about what they wear as long as they aren't walking around naked in the street. Some like to talk on the telephone a lot; others don't like making or receiving telephone calls. Some like to eat in restaurants; others prefer to eat at home. None of these things are better or worse than the others. They are different ways of doing things.

When I talked about the old saying, "When in Rome, do as the Romans do," I suggested that you try to do things the way others do if you want to get along with them. I also said that you shouldn't have to do things their way *all the time*. There are times when it's only fair that others do things your way. For example, if you move into the house where your stepsiblings have lived before, you shouldn't have to do everything their way just because it's their house. Also, if your stepsiblings are the ones who have moved into your house, you can't tell them to do things your way just because they're new there. If you both are moving into a new place, you' will both have to give up some old ways and work out new ways together.

So when you first move in together with your stepsiblings, it's important to remember that there are bound to be things that you will be doing differently from them. The best thing you can do is to talk with them about the differences. In many cases, it really shouldn't make a difference which way something is done, your way or theirs. As long as their way doesn't *really* bother you and as long as your way doesn't *really* bother them, you should each respect the other's way of doing things.

For example, if you like to read books a lot and your stepbrother is very much into sports, there's no reason why each of you shouldn't be free to do your "own thing." Your reading shouldn't bother him, and his playing baseball shouldn't bother you.

There will, however, be some different ways of doing things that affect everybody. If, for example, your stepsiblings like certain foods that you don't, it's a good idea to tell whoever is doing the cooking which foods you like and which ones you don't like. Then there can be days when food that you prefer will be served and other days when everyone will get the food that others prefer. The days can be rotated so that every day a different person has first choice.

Following the Rules of the House Another thing that has to happen if there is to be less fighting among stepsiblings is that everyone has to agree to make more rules and follow them. The more people there are living together, the more rules they need. Sometimes these may even be written down and posted on a wall or on the refrigerator. The rules may involve the different chores that each person is assigned to do and the days on which they must be done. There may be rules about bedtime and about curfews, that is, the times when children have to be home in the afternoon or evening. There have to be rules about when different people can use the bathroom, or else there will be a lot of fighting in the morning. There have to be rules about television, not only concerning how much time children can spend watching it but how to rotate who gets first choice of program and on which days. There also have

to be rules about what should be served at mealtimes so that everyone gets a chance to have his or her favorite foods. The more people agree on, and follow, the rules, the more peace and harmony there will be in the house, and the happier everyone will be.

Sometimes there will still be trouble even though rules have been made. Then everyone has to sit down and think of a way of solving the problem. For example, in one stepfamily home, there were four children of different ages—two teenagers and two younger children. No matter how hard everyone tried, they still had fights about television. They could never agree on which program to watch. The teenagers, especially, didn't like the programs the younger children liked. So they made a rule that one day the teenagers should decide which programs they wanted to watch, and the

146

next day the younger children would have first choice. But even this didn't work because sometimes the teenagers couldn't agree between themselves, and sometimes the two younger children couldn't agree.

Finally, one of the younger children got a good idea. She had seen a special sale on television sets in one of the stores near where they lived. It was a small set and it cost seventy-five dollars, which is cheap for a television set. Why couldn't everyone chip in to buy the set? People could save up from their allowances and also earn extra money by doing chores for neighbors. The children discussed this with their parents, who also thought it was a good idea. In fact, the parents thought it was such a good idea that they decided to donate thirty-five dollars to the purchase of the set. Therefore, each child had to put in ten dollars. It took about a month until all the children had saved up enough money. There was a lot of hard work involved, but after they got the new set, everyone agreed it was worth the effort. Now, with two television sets in the house, there was far less fighting over what programs to watch.

Family Meetings Family meetings can be very helpful in avoiding and solving problems among stepsiblings. At these meetings, both the parents and the children should be present. The purpose of the meeting is to solve problems among the stepsiblings as well as between the children and the parents. Some people call these "gripe sessions" or "rap sessions." In some families, they are held only when there is a special problem. In other families, they are held at certain times, like once every week on a specific day. This is one of the best ways to avoid family problems as well as solving them. At such meetings, everyone can have a say and make suggestions for dealing with the problem.

In one family, a boy named Harry refused to take the garbage out every time it was his turn. Others complained about this at the family meeting. When Harry was asked why he wasn't taking out the garbage, he just said things like "I was tired" or "I forgot." The others all thought that this was a "cop-out," that Harry was just being lazy and wanted to get out of doing his job. After discussing the different things that might be done, the others voted that Harry could not watch television until *after* he had taken out the garbage. This helped Harry remember to do his job, and there was no trouble about it from then on.

In another stepfamily, Roberta, Julie, and Fran often baked a cake or cookies together. They not only had a lot of fun making them, but they loved eating what they had made. Most of all, they liked seeing how much everyone else enjoyed eating what they had cooked. However, Julie and Fran had one big complaint about Roberta. She refused to help clean up the mess after they had finished with the baking. No matter how much they would ask her to help, she refused. Finally, they discussed the problem at a family meeting. Roberta simply said that she liked to bake things but that she hated to clean up afterward. Everybody explained to her that there are times when you have to do things you don't like if you're going to be allowed to do the things you do like. Everyone told her that the two things often go together—the good part and the bad

148

part. Roberta just answered, "I don't want to have anything to do with the bad part." Because they couldn't convince Roberta to change her mind, the family voted that Roberta would not be allowed to eat any of the cake and cookies until *after* she had cleaned up. They also decided that if Roberta didn't cooperate, her mother would come in to be sure that Roberta did not get any cake or cookies until she helped clean up the mess. After this discusssion, the problem was solved. Roberta knew that everyone was serious and that there would be no cake or cookies for her if she didn't help clean up. The family meeting worked well for this stepfamily.

Your Stepsiblings Aren't the Only People in the World You Can Spend Time With Another thing that can help reduce fighting among stepsiblings is for each child to remember that you don't have to love or even like your stepsiblings. Just as you don't necessarily have to like or love a stepparent, you don't have to like or love a stepsibling. Of course, it is nicer when people try to like one another and do things to get along better. But even when everyone tries hard, there may still be some children who just do not like a stepsibling. A child who likes sports a lot may have little in common with a stepsibling who likes reading and studying. One child may like indoor board and table games; another may like outdoor games. One may like to build models; another may like stamp and coin collecting. One may like to listen to music a lot; another may just like silence. No one can like everything about another person. No two people like doing all the exact same things.

If you find that there are very few things that you like doing with your stepsiblings, it is important to remember that they are not the only children in the world. There are many other children who enjoy doing the same things you do. There are many other children besides your stepsiblings with whom you can be friendly and have good times. So if this is your situation, it is a good idea to go and find out where these children are. Some are likely to live in your neighborhood. Some may be found in school, both in your classes and in after-school clubs. In fact, after-school clubs are an especially good place to meet children with your interests because those who join know in advance what they will be doing. For example, if you are interested in stamp collecting, it's a good idea to join a club with other children who have the same interest. If there isn't

such a club in your school, there may be one at a "Y" or recreational center near you.

The most important thing to remember is that these other children are not going to come to you. You have to go out and find where they are. There is no question that there are friends for everyone, but you have to go out and find them. You can't just sit on your backside and expect them to come to you.

What I have just said about getting friends is true about most of the other things I talk about in this book. Good things don't just happen to people who sit and do nothing. The best things happen to people who go out and do things and work toward the goals they want to achieve.

Half Siblings A half sibling is the child of your natural parent and your stepparent. A half sibling is halfway between a full sibling and a stepsibling. Stepsiblings may cause problems, but they can often help make your life happier. In the same way, half siblings can cause problems, but they can also help you become happier.

Having Children Is the Parents' Decision, Not the Child's When children with stepsiblings think about the possibility that a parent and stepparent will have another child, they are usually upset. "There are enough kids around already," they may say. "Who wants more?" Of course, the answer to that question is: the parent and the stepparent. If they love one another very much, it's natural for them to want a child who is both of theirs. As much as each may love the stepchildren, it is common to want one or more children in the new marriage. This is especially true if the parent and stepparent are still young. A stepparent who has never had any children before is especially likely to want one of his or her own.

If your parent and stepparent are talking about having a child, there is really nothing you can do about it. The decision is theirs, not yours. Although it is a good idea to tell them your thoughts and feelings about having a new brother or sister, they, and only they, should make the final decision. Parents should ask children about their feelings and thoughts about a new baby coming into the home, but they should not leave the decision to the children. What the children say might be useful to them in helping them make their decision, but the final decision should be the parents'. I hope you realize this if your parents have asked you how you would feel about a new baby.

Sometimes, however, a parent will ask a child for his or her opinion and even say that if the child feels strongly that there should be no other children, then there will be none. In other words, the parent and stepparent are leaving the decision to the child. I think this is a big mistake. Even the smartest children just don't have enough knowledge and experience to tell their parents whether or not to have more children. And it is unfair for parents to give this much responsibility to a child. What if the parents really want another baby and then follow a child's advice not to? Those parents may be depriving themselves of the great joys of having a child just because the older children feel jealous. But all children are jealous at times, and this is

152

not a good reason for not having other children. So if your parents have told you that it will be your decision—and they really mean it—try to show them what I have just said here: that the decision should be theirs not yours.

Most children don't like the idea of a new baby coming into the home. If the decision were up to them, they would usually vote no. This is also true of children whose parents have never been divorced. Most children have enough sharing already, and they don't want to share any more. But the parents have the right to have more children anyway, because of the pleasures children can give them. The older children have to learn to accept the new baby. And they have to learn that good things can come from its being in the home, not only bad things. I will talk more about these good things later.

Fears Children Have About Half Siblings One of the biggest fears stepchildren have is that the stepmother will love the new baby, the half sibling, more than she loves them. This is a reasonable fear to have. After all, the new baby is a *blood* relative of the stepparent, and the stepchildren are not. As I have said before, a stepparent probably will love his or her own child more than a stepchild at first. However, as I have also said, a stepparent *can* come to love a stepchild as much as a natural child. This is more likely to happen if the stepparent and stepchild are kind to one another over a long time. The best you can do to make this happen is to be friendly and try to have a good relationship with your stepparent. Then there is a greater chance that

your stepparent will come to love you and less of a chance that the stepparent will love the new baby more.

Another fear children have about half siblings is that the natural parent will love the half sibling more than the children from the previous marriage. Although the fear that a stepparent will love the half sibling more is reasonable, this fear is not. Your natural parent has the same blood tie to you as he or she has to your new half sibling. If your mother has a new baby, both you and the new baby have been born from her body. You and the new baby have different fathers but the same mother. To her, you and the new baby are both her children, and there is no good reason why she shouldn't love both of you equally. If your father's new wife has a baby, that child is as closely related to your father as you are. Both of you come from his sperm. To him you are both his own children. There is no reason why he should love you any less than the new baby.

If you worry that your stepparent or your natural parent loves your half sibling more than you, talk to them about it. Often, this will help you decide whether it is only your imagination or whether they really love the half sibling more than you. It is not only what your parent and stepparent *say* that should help you decide, but also what they *do*. See if they treat you any differently from the half sibling. Of course, a new baby requires more care and attention than older children, but this doesn't mean that the parent or stepparent loves you less. See how they are when they are with you. See if they enjoy being with you. See if they are proud of the things you do and say. See if they take care of you when there is trouble. See if they are interested in the things you do, both at home and in school. See if they are sure to buy presents for all the children, both natural and step, when there are special occasions like birthdays and holidays. See if they are sure to be fair and give the same kinds of punishments when someone is bad. See if they don't forget anyone when they give out cookies, or ice cream, or other good things that children like. If they are doing all these things most of the time, then they love you. This is true even if they spend more time with the new baby than they spend with you.

It is also important to remember that some people don't talk about their loving feelings as easily as others. This does not necessarily mean that they are less loving; it may only mean that they express their love more by the things they do than by what they say. A father

155

might not *talk* much, if at all, about how much he loves his children, but he is always *doing* things for them like taking them on trips, making their lunches, helping with their projects, and shining their shoes. All these things prove to the children that he loves them. A mother, also, may not say much about how she loves her children, but she may work very hard every day doing things for them. She may get up early to prepare breakfast for them, she may cook their favorite foods, and she may worry a lot about them when they are sick and spend long hours trying to help them get better. All these things prove that she is devoted and loving even though she may not often say that she loves them. So remember that the important thing is what people *do* to prove their love, not so much what they say.

How Half Siblings Can Help Make Your Home a Happier Place In a way, a new stepfamily is just like two separate families living together in the same home. No one is a blood relative of anyone else. When a half sibling is born, the new baby is everyone's blood relative. It is a blood relative of the mother and father because they are the parents of the child, and it is a blood relative of all the other children of the mother and father. If the baby is a girl, she is a half sister to all the natural children and stepchildren. And if the baby is a boy, he is a half brother to all the siblings and stepsiblings.

So the baby helps bring everybody closer together. It helps link and tie the relationships among the various people. Now everyone in the family is more closely related to one another. This is one of the ways a half

156

sibling can help make people feel closer and be happier with one another.

Although the baby takes up room and although it also takes a lot of the parents' time, the baby can be a source of great pleasure to everyone. Babies can be a lot of fun to hold and cuddle. Although they sometimes cry, they also laugh a lot and make people feel good inside. Babies bring people joy because they are so cute and friendly. Most people like cuddling babies, bouncing them up and down, and kissing them. This is another way that half siblings can make families happier.

As I have mentioned, many children fear that the stepfamily will break up as well. The children's parents have been divorced before, and they may fear that they will get divorced again. In a stepfamily, the parents usually try to be very sure that they are getting along

very well before they have another child together. When a half sibling is born, it usually means that the parents are getting along quite well together. In addition, the new baby brings the parents even closer and lessens the chances that there will be another divorce. I am not saying that it is impossible for there to be a divorce after a half sibling is born. I *am* saying that it becomes less likely. There is a great possibility that everyone will be even closer to one another.

8
ADOPTION BY A STEPPARENT

First I would like to tell you what adoption means, because some of the children reading this may not know the meaning of the word. I have told you about natural or real parents, and I have told you about stepparents. In a way, an adoptive parent is halfway between a natural parent and a stepparent. I can best explain this by talking first about adopted babies, which most of you probably do know about. In fact, I am sure that some of you who are reading this book are adopted children.

Sometimes a man and woman cannot have children of their own. For some reason, a baby won't start growing in the woman's belly, or the man's sperm won't start one growing. The two people may then get a baby from someone else. Often, it is a baby of a woman who is not married and does not wish to or cannot take care of the baby after it is born. Lawyers then fill out certain papers, and a judge decides that the baby will no longer belong to the woman who had the baby but can be given to the man and woman who have asked to have the baby. The baby is then said to have been *adopted* by the man and woman. They are called the *adoptive* parents. The natural mother does not take care of the baby anymore. In fact, she *cannot* live with the child anymore. She cannot be involved with taking care of it. She cannot even see the child unless the adoptive parents want her to, and they usually don't. Usually, the child never sees the original mother again and goes through life never even knowing what the natural mother looked like. Such children just know the adoptive parents as the only parents they can ever remember.

What is important about adoptive parents is that they have the full responsibility of caring for the child. They pay for its food, clothing, and the home in which they live with the child. They raise it themselves and have full control over what happens to the child. The parent who has given the child up has no control over what happens to the child and does not have to pay for its food, clothing, or the home where it lives. The adoptive parent has all the rights and powers of a real parent. The parent who has given up the child has no rights or responsibilities. Even though the natural parent is still a blood relative, that parent becomes a stranger or totally unknown to the child.

There is another kind of adoption. It is the kind that can take place in stepfamilies. In this kind of adoption, the natural parent gives up the child to the stepparent. The natural parent no longer takes care of the child or sends money for its support. However, the natural parent then has absolutely no say at all regarding what happens to the child and has no control over it. The adoptive stepparent takes care of the child, supports it, and has total control over what happens to it. The adoptive stepparent is no longer even called a stepparent. He or she is called the adoptive parent or, often, just the parent. If the adoptive stepparent is a man, the child then changes his or her last name to that of the adoptive stepparent. If the adoptive stepparent is a woman, then the child does not change his or her last name because the child already has the last name of the father with whom he or she is living. The adoptive parent, then, is closer than a stepparent but not as close a relative as a real parent. That is why I say that an adoptive parent is halfway between a natural parent and a stepparent.

Most children who live in stepfamilies still visit with the natural parent with whom they are not living. Most natural parents still want to see their children very often even though they may not be living with them. In such situations, the question of adoption does not arise. For example, Sarah lives with her mother and her stepfather Henry. Sarah loves her father very much, and he loves her very much as well. Sarah sees her father often. She also loves Henry and feels that she is luckier than some of her friends, whose stepfathers are not as nice. Even though she loves her father, she also loves Henry. As I have said before, it doesn't have to be a choice between loving a parent and a stepparent. You can love both. Also, Sarah's mother and Henry get along very well and hardly ever fight. The question of Henry's adopting Sarah has never come up. Sarah always wants to be her father's daughter. Sarah's father always wants Sarah to be his daughter. And Henry, although he loves Sarah, knows that it's best for Sarah to still remain the daughter of her natural father even though she lives with him.

There are times, however, when the parent who does not live with a child has little, if any, love for the child. Such a parent may hardly ever visit, call, or write, or even think about the child. This parent may not send the money he or she is supposed to, money to help support the child. It is sad to say, but a parent who acts this way does not love the child. In this situation, a stepparent may wish to adopt the child. Even though the stepparent is already treating the child as if he or she were his or her own son or daughter, adoption can bring them even closer.

This was Ann and Larry Norton's situation. Even when their mother and father were married, they saw little of their father. He would come home very late and leave early in the morning. Sometimes Mr. Norton wouldn't come home at all. Their parents used to fight a lot because their father showed so little interest in their mother and the two children. Finally, their parents separated and got a divorce. After their father left the house, they never saw him again. He moved to a nearby town but never visited, called, or wrote. He never sent their mother money. He never even sent his children a birthday card or present. It didn't take Ann and Larry long to get used to the idea that their father didn't love them. That made them sad, but they knew their mother and other relatives loved them, and that helped make them feel better.

About a year after their parents divorced, their mother married Mark Taylor, a man whose wife had died. Mark had a son, Fred, who got along very well with Ann and Larry even though they did fight, bicker, and tease once in a while. Mark Taylor treated Ann and

162

Larry very well, and as time passed, they came to love one another deeply. Finally, Ann and Larry felt as if Mark were their real father, and they nearly forgot about their natural father.

One day, Mark and their mother asked the children if they would like to be adopted by Mark. They said that they would like that very much, especially since they already felt as if Mark were their father anyway. There was no trouble getting their real father to give his permission. He had no interest in the children and was happy that someone else wanted the responsibility of raising them. They got a lawyer who wrote out some papers. Then everyone went to court, and the judge said that Ann and Larry would be Mark's children from then on. On that day, their last name was changed from Norton to Taylor. This made them even happier.

Sometimes things are not as simple as they were for Ann and Larry. Their natural father quickly gave permission for the adoption, and so there was no problem. If the natural father does not wish to give permission, then the children may not be able to be adopted by a stepparent. It's up to the judge to decide. Even if the parent has no love or interest in the children, and even if the parent hardly ever visits or sends money, that parent can still prevent children from being adopted by someone else. This is what happened to Nora and James. They lived with their mother and their stepfather, Ned. Ned had never been married before and had no children. He loved Nora and James very much and felt as if they were his own children. Nora and James's father had left home one day many years before and never visited, called, wrote, or sent money even though he lived in the same town. The children certainly did not feel that he was their father anymore. They loved Ned and felt as if he were their father.

When Ned wanted to adopt the children, everyone was very happy—everyone except their natural father. Even though he had no interest in the children and certainly could not be said to love them, he still wouldn't give his permission. They took the case to court, and the judge ruled that the children could not be adopted by Ned because their father came and told the judge that he would not give his permission. He was being mean and thinking only about his own feelings, but there was nothing that anyone could do. Although Ned still remained their stepfather, they still felt as if he were their real father. They would have been happier if the judge had let Ned adopt them, but it didn't affect their lives too much that he hadn't. They still enjoyed living with and loving Ned and were very glad that their mother had married him. They felt lucky, too. Some of their friends whose parents had gotten divorced either ended up without a second parent or a stepparent whom they didn't like.

Sometimes natural parents will give up children for adoption and say they really love the children very much and are just letting them be adopted because it's best for them. This is what happened to George. His mother left home, and he remained living with his father. She visited once in a while, but George never knew in advance when she would be coming, and she never stayed very long. George and his father knew that she really didn't like visiting with him very much and just came because she felt guilty at times. She hardly ever called him on the phone, and when George called her, she often wasn't home. In fact, she would often go away for weeks and he wouldn't know where she was. George gradually realized that his mother had very little love for him. This, of course, made him very sad. However, he gradually felt better as he spent time with other people, both young and old, who did love him.

Then his father met a very nice woman named Gail. She had never been married before and had never had any children. From the beginning, she and George liked one another. After a while, Gail moved into the house with George and his father to see whether she and George's father should get married. After living together for about six months, they found that they loved one another even more, and so they got married.

George and Gail came to love one another very much as well. After Gail moved in with George's father, George saw even less of his mother.

Finally, one day, George's mother came to visit. She, George's father, and Gail sat down with George and talked with him about his thoughts and feelings about being adopted by Gail. Gail wanted to do this very much, and George's father was also in favor of the plan. George also liked the idea. When George's mother was asked her opinion, she replied, "George, I really love you very much. I think you know that. Although I really don't want to give you up, I think it would be best for you if Gail adopted you. In fact, it would probably be best if I removed myself from you and your new family entirely. Then I won't be an interference. For your sake, I'm going to give my permission for Gail to adopt you. And, for your sake, I'm going to gradually remove myself entirely and stop seeing you."

George did not believe for one minute that his mother loved him. For a few years now, she had hardly seen him. He did not believe that she was giving him up for adoption for his sake, as a favor to him. He believed that his mother was happy to get rid of him. He believed that she was only saying she was giving him up for his sake so that she wouldn't feel guilty about what she was doing. George told his mother what he felt. He told her that she was lying when she said she was giving him up for his sake. He also told her that he was happy that she was giving permission for Gail to adopt him because he loved Gail, Gail loved him, and he really felt that Gail was more of a mother to him than she was.

George's mother was surprised to hear what George

was saying. Although she was ashamed to admit it, she knew that what George was saying was true. Both she and George began to cry. Both agreed that it had been good to be honest with one another even though the things they had said had been painful for both of them. And so George's mother left the house. The adoption took place, and he hardly ever saw his mother again. He was happy in his new home and did not miss her very much.

9
IF YOU NEED MORE HELP

If you have a problem, the first thing you should try to do is solve it yourself. If the trouble is with another person, then it's best to talk to that person and try to solve the problem together. Getting advice from books like this is another way of dealing with problems. However, there are some problems that may be very difficult to solve. In such cases, a therapist may help.

A therapist is a person who tries to help people who have troubles, worries, or problems. I say *tries* because sometimes the therapist can help people and sometimes the therapist cannot. One of the most important things that determines whether a therapist can help a person is whether the person wants to be helped and tries hard to change. Many people go to a therapist and think that by just going there things are going to get better. It doesn't work that way. If you go to school and just sit and don't listen to what the teacher says and don't try to hear what she or he is saying, you're not going to learn very much in school. In the same way, if you go to a therapist and don't try to solve your problems, you're not going to be helped very much. In fact, you probably won't be helped at all.

WHO SHOULD SEE A THERAPIST?

Not everybody should see a therapist. As I have said, it's best to try to solve problems yourself. Only when you have tried many times, and in many different ways, should you go to a therapist. Perhaps you are wondering exactly what kinds of problems a therapist can help you with and when you should ask for help.

If there is almost continual fighting in a stepfamily, or if discussions and family meetings can't help solve a problem, then it might be a good idea to seek the help of a therapist. Sometimes only one person has to see the therapist. Sometimes more than one. If two people always seem to be having trouble with one another, then it is often useful for both to see the therapist together. If only one goes, the problem between them may not be helped.

Many stepfamily problems involve a number of people. In such cases, it can be useful for all the people involved in the problem at attend. It's like having a family meeting with an additional person to lead and be involved in the discussion. Because the therapist has met with many families, he knows the kinds of problems people in stepfamilies have. Because he isn't personally involved in the problems, he can think more clearly about them than the members of the family. We can never see ourselves the way an outsider can. People in our own family may not see us as clearly as a stranger. When there are all kinds of feelings like love, hate, and fear, we cannot think clearly about ourselves and others. Another person, who does not have all these feelings so strongly, can see the situation more

clearly and may be in a better position than we are to help solve our problems.

No one should be forced to go to a therapist. But sometimes a child doesn't want to go, and the parents may insist that he or she go a few times. I think this is perfectly all right. In fact, I myself sometimes suggest this to parents. You cannot know what you are saying no to until you go and find out what it is. After a child has gone a few times and actually seen what therapy is like, then he or she is in a better position to decide whether or not to go. Without being there, you cannot really know whether or not you like it. Some of the children who have been forced to go are happy later that they were forced because they have been helped with their problems. If they had not been forced, they would never have gone, and they would not have been helped.

170

WHAT HAPPENS WHEN YOU SEE A THERAPIST?

Therapists do many kinds of things, and different therapists work differently. The kind of therapist I have been talking about here tries to help people with their problems by talking about them. They try to help people see things more clearly. They try to help people figure out solutions to their problems. They may tell people about the things they are doing that are adding to their troubles, things that the people may not even realize they are doing. They may suggest different ways of dealing with troubles, ways that are less likely to cause difficulty, or ways that may solve the problem entirely. Sometimes a therapist sees only one person in a family and sometimes more than one. As I have said, if more than one person is involved in a problem, then all the involved people should see the therapist. I think that this is the best way to solve a problem that involves more than one person.

Sometimes therapists play games with the children they see. The best therapists play special kinds of games that help children learn about their problems. Some therapists spend a lot of time playing such games as checkers or chess with children or build models with them. I myself do not think that this kind of therapy is too useful. Games in which children make up stories are, in my opinion, much more useful. Dolls, puppets, drawings, and tape recorders are often used to help children make up stories. From these made-up stories, the therapist can learn a lot about what's bothering a person. There are still other games, games that don't involve storytelling, that therapists use to help children talk about the things that are bothering them. These special games are also very useful in therapy.

A therapist may ask you about your dreams. Did you know that our dreams can tell us a lot about what our most important problems and feelings are? A dream can also give a lot of information about what's troubling a person. It's best that the person try to figure out what the dream means, what it is telling the dreamer about him- or herself. But it's often hard to figure out the meaning of our own dreams by ourselves. Many therapists have learned how to help people figure out their dreams. It's almost like cracking a secret code. The decoded information can be very useful in helping people solve their problems.

Some therapists also give pills. Most of the problems that I have spoken about in this book are not the kinds for which I give pills. Some therapists do give pills for these kinds of troubles. Often, the people who take them are looking for quick and easy solutions to their problems. Most of the problems that people have in stepfamilies are not easy to solve and are not helped by pills. At best, pills might make a person a little calmer. I am not saying that I never suggest pills for the kinds of problems discussed in this book. I am only saying that I hardly ever do. I believe that learning about what's wrong and working toward doing something about your troubles are much more likely to help.

THERE'S NOTHING TO BE ASHAMED ABOUT IF YOU GO TO A THERAPIST

There was a time when many people were ashamed to see a therapist. However, as time has passed, more and more people have come to realize that there is nothing to be ashamed about. Everybody has troubles from time to time. No one goes through life without having any problems at all.

Some children who see a therapist try to keep it a big secret. I think it's perfectly all right to have some privacy and not let everyone know all your business. But if you are sneaking around fearful that someone will find out where you're going, then you're adding a new problem to the ones you already have. The main thing that other children are interested in is the kind of person you are. If you are nice to others and fun to be with, then it won't matter to them that you're seeing a therapist. If you're mean and selfish and no fun to be with, then others will not want to be with you even if you aren't seeing a therapist. The important thing is what kind of person you are. That determines whether people will like you, not whether you are seeing a therapist.

YOU DON'T HAVE TO BE CRAZY
TO SEE A THERAPIST

There are still some people who think that only crazy people go to therapists. They won't go to one because they think that if they do, it will mean that they are crazy. This is a wrong idea. Most of the people therapists see are considered normal by others who meet them. They just have problems over certain things they do or say. No one can tell, as they walk down the street, that they are seeing a therapist. They don't look any different from everyday people. All normal people have some kinds of problems. There is no one who cannot be helped at some time in his or her life by seeing a therapist. So just because you may be seeing a therapist does not mean you are sick. This is also true of other members of your family who may also be seeing a therapist.

The people who are really sick are usually the ones who won't go. They are so sick that they may not recognize that they have problems. The person who does go is usually healthy and normal enough to realize that he or she has problems. That person also has the strength to face unpleasant things about him- or herself. Crazy people often don't want to see a therapist because they are much too frightened of the truth and can't face unpleasant things about themselves.

Unfortunately, there are some children who are seeing therapists who are called names like "crazy," or "retard," or "mental." The children who are called such names are hardly ever sick or retarded. There is, however, something wrong with the children who are calling them names. They are being cruel and mean. They often have some problems of their own. If you are going to a therapist, and this happens to you, remember that there is probably something wrong with anyone who calls you these names. Sometimes it's best to ignore such name-callers. Sometimes it's best to call them names back. Sometimes it's best to tell them that there must be something wrong with them.

There are some children with only a few problems who do not believe what I have said about craziness and going to a therapist. Even after reading what I have said—that going to a therapist does not mean that you are crazy—they still believe it. Because of this, they will not go, or they may go once and quit—even though the therapist has told them personally that they are not crazy. This is very sad. These children may find it difficult to solve their problems. They may remain unhappy. Had they gone, they might have solved their problems. They might then have been much happier.

10
SOME IMPORTANT THINGS
TO REMEMBER

I have said many things in this book that I hope will be helpful to children living in stepfamilies. No one's memory is good enough to remember them all. So I hope you will read over, from time to time, the parts that talk about things that are happening to you. It's a good idea to read along with a parent or stepparent, and to talk together about the things I have said. This is the best way to solve problems and to make life in a stepfamily happier.

Here are some especially important things to remember—

Everybody is a mixture of good and bad parts. This is true of you and me, of mothers and fathers, and of stepmothers and stepfathers.

Love is not like the "on-off" electric light switch. It's more like the dimmer. Toward any person, we may feel no love at all, a little bit of love, a lot of love, or great amounts of love. The more loving things a person does, the more likely we will love him or her.

176

Although it's nicer if you love a stepparent, it isn't necessary to love him or her. Although it's nicer if a stepparent loves you, it isn't necessary that a stepparent love a stepchild. The more everyone works at it, the more likely it is that loving feelings will grow.

A stepparent does not necessarily have to be mean and cruel.

If somebody does things that bother you and make you angry, talk with that person about what's bothering you. If you do this, there's some chance that the problem will be solved. If you don't do this, it's not likely that the person will stop doing the things that are bothering you. Remember the old saying "Nothing ventured, nothing gained."

Remember the lesson that King Pyrrhus learned a long time ago: there are some wars that nobody really wins. Both sides lose.

If you're having an argument with a stepparent and your parent doesn't take your side, it doesn't mean that your parent doesn't love you.

Sharing is very important if there is to be peace in a stepfamily.

If you think that you'll be unhappy in a stepfamily, remember that it can be another chance to have a complete family living all together. And this can make your life happier.

THE STORY OF THE PHOENIX

Before ending this book, I'd like to tell you about the phoenix (sounds like: FEE-nix). Thousands of years ago, in Egypt, Arabia, India, and many other countries in that part of the world, a story was told about a bird called a phoenix. It was told over and over again. Parents told their children, and when the children grew up, they told their children, and so on down the years. Such a story is called a legend. Actually, there never really was a bird called a phoenix. It was a make-believe bird.

According to the legend, a phoenix lived a certain number of years, usually about five-hundred. Just before it was about to die, it built a nest of twigs on which it placed spices. It then sang a sad song about dying. Next, the phoenix set fire to its own nest, and while sitting on the burning twigs, it flapped its wings so that the flames would get bigger and bigger. In this way, it burned itself to death.

However, that is not the end of the story. After the phoenix was completely burned to ashes, it rose again as a young bird that was formed from its own ashes. The phoenix was born again and went on to live another life.

As I have said, there never was a real phoenix. There never was a bird that was born again from its own dead ashes. However, the legend lives, and the bird has come to stand for something that is born again, something that was dead and has come back to life. For example, there is a city in the state of Arizona called Phoenix. It was built in the middle of

178

a great desert. From a distance, it looks as if it rose out of the desert, from the dead desert sands. Like the phoenix, something alive has grown out of something dead.

Now you may be wondering why I have decided to end this book by talking about the phoenix. Some of you may already have guessed why. The reason is that a new marriage can be like a phoenix. The old marriage has died, and the new marriage, with all the children, can be a new family formed from the parts of the old. It can be a new life to take the place of the old. However, it doesn't just happen. It doesn't just turn into a happy family all by itself. The people in it, both young and old, have to work toward making it a good and a happy family. If you want it very badly and try

hard, it is possible that you can make your new family into a loving and happy one. Then, like the phoenix, a new life will have been born from the old one. I hope that this book will help you make such a new family.

ABOUT THE AUTHOR

Richard A. Gardner, M.D., a practicing child psychiatrist and adult psychoanalyst, is Clinical Professor of Child Psychiatry at the Columbia University, College of Physicians and Surgeons. He was formerly a faculty member of the William A. White Psychoanalytic Institute and a Visiting Professor of Child Psychiatry at the University of Louvain in Belgium. He has written extensively for children, parents, and professionals in the field of child psychiatry—where he is recognized as one of the leading innovators in the field. His *Mutual Storytelling Technique* and his *Talking, Feeling, and Doing Game* have become standard instruments in child psychotherapy.

Dr. Gardner is certified in psychiatry and child psychiatry by the American Board of Psychiatry and Neurology. He is a Fellow of the American Psychiatric Association, the American Academy of Child Psychiatry, and the American Academy of Psychoanalysis. He is listed in *Contemporary Authors, Who's Who in America,* and *Who's Who in the World.*

Books and Diagnostic/Therapeutic Instruments by Richard A. Gardner, M.D.

Title	Unit Price		Quantity	Total
The Talking, Feeling, and Doing Game	19	75		
The Boys and Girls Book About Divorce (Paperback)	2	95		
The Parents Book About Divorce (Paperback)	3	95		
The Boys and Girls Book About One-Parent Families (Paperback)	2	95		
The Boys and Girls Book About Stepfamilies (Paperback)	2	95		
Psychotherapy with Children of Divorce	40	00		
Family Evaluation in Child Custody Litigation	19	75		
The Objective Diagnosis of Minimal Brain Dysfunction	18	75		
The Reversals Frequency Test	12	00		
MBD: The Family Book About Minimal Brain Dysfunction	20	00		
Therapeutic Communication with Children: The Mutual Storytelling Technique	40	00		
Psychotherapeutic Approaches to the Resistant Child	35	00		
Dr. Gardner's Stories About the Real World, Vol. I	8	25		
Dr. Gardner's Stories About the Real World, Vol. I (Paperback)	2	95		
Dr. Gardner's Stories About the Real World, Vol. II	9	95		
Dr. Gardner's Fairy Tales for Today's Children	8	25		
Dr. Gardner's Modern Fairy Tales	8	25		
Dorothy and the Lizard of Oz	9	95		
Dr. Gardner's Fables for Our Times	10	95		
Understanding Children — A Parents Guide to Child Rearing	12	50		
The Adoption Story Cards	12	00		
Separation Anxiety Disorder: Psychodynamics and Psychotherapy	15	95		
Child Custody Litigation – A Guidebook for Parents and Therapists (publ. 1986)	18	00		

	Subtotal	

$2.00 for orders under $10.00
$2.50 for orders between $10.01 and $35.00 } . . . . Postage and handling
8% of subtotal for orders over $35.00

New Jersey residents add 6% of subtotal for sales tax
*Canadian and foreign orders for **The Talking, Feeling, and Doing Game**
add $4.50 per game to the postage and handling charge

Total of Order

FULL PAYMENT MUST ACCOMPANY ORDER
*Canadian and foreign checks must be drawn in U.S. dollars from a U.S. Bank.

Name _____

Facility _____

Address _____

City _____ State _____ Zip _____

Send check to: **CREATIVE THERAPEUTICS, P.O. Box R, Cresskill, NJ 07626–0317**